Hands clamped at Calvin James's arms

James's fingers slipped from the frame of his Smith & Wesson chopper, and the gun fell to the floor.

Suddenly, a streak of yellow flashed past James's eyes and he felt a garrote close around his throat. Another Thuggee had got behind him and applied his deadly strangler skills. The other two fanatics still held on to James's arms as the killer tightened the cord around the Phoenix warrior's neck.

A terrible pressure dug into the black man's windpipe as the knot containing a silver rupee threatened to crush his Adam's apple....

Mack Bolan's
PHOENIX FORCE

#1 Argentine Deadline
#2 Guerilla Games
#3 Atlantic Scramble
#4 Tigers of Justice
#5 The Fury Bombs
#6 White Hell
#7 Dragon's Kill
#8 Aswan Hellbox
#9 Ultimate Terror
#10 Korean Killground
#11 Return to Armageddon
#12 The Black Alchemists
#13 Harvest Hell
#14 Phoenix in Flames
#15 The Viper Factor
#16 No Rules, No Referee
#17 Welcome to the Feast
#18 Night of the Thuggee

PHOENIX FORCE
Night of the Thuggee

Gar Wilson

A GOLD EAGLE BOOK FROM
W🌐RLDWIDE

TORONTO · NEW YORK · LONDON · PARIS
AMSTERDAM · STOCKHOLM · HAMBURG
ATHENS · MILAN · TOKYO · SYDNEY

First edition July 1985

ISBN 0-373-61318-0

Special thanks and acknowledgment to
William Fieldhouse for his contributions to this work.

Printed in Canada

1

Edward Ashley waited at the corner for a tram when he felt something tug his pant cuff. He instinctively shoved a hand in his pocket to guard his wallet. New Delhi, like any other large city, has its share of thieves. Pickpockets like to work in crowds, and the streets of New Delhi are always crowded.

Ashley glanced down and saw his trousers were snared on a long dark horn. He pulled away from the cow. Dull brown eyes gazed up at him. The beast lay on the sidewalk, calmly chewing its cud and shooing away flies with its tail.

"Bloody brute," Ashley muttered as he examined the tear in his pants.

A former sergeant major in the British Army, Edward Ashley had seen a good deal of the world and lived among several different cultures, but none baffled him more than India. It was dreadfully overpopulated. Poverty and starvation were commonplace. Yet sacred cows still wandered about the streets, and the Hindus were horrified if anyone suggested that some of these animals be turned into unholy hamburger.

Of course, the Hindus consider all life to be sacred. Ashley wondered why so many of those chaps did not seem to feel as much concern for malnourished children and emaciated old beggers as they did for bleedin' cows and monkeys. Quality of life has never been a high priority in India. Animals are supposed to do what nature intended, and people...well, they're supposed to concentrate on spiritual matters.

Ashley had cynically noticed that the Brahman priests were at the head of the Indian caste system along with the Kshatriya aristocrats. He did not find it surprising that the Hindu religion continued to endorse the caste system that, despite efforts at social reform, was still very much a part of India.

However, Ashley did not understand the philosophy of Hinduism, which teaches that all things run in cycles. One dies and moves on to another incarnation. If one's deeds were favorable in the past life, then the laws of karma meant the soul would be reborn to a higher caste. If one has led an evil life, he will be reincarnated to a lower caste. Thus to the Hindu the caste system is necessary for the balance of the universe and divine justice.

Hinduism has little concern for science or modern technology. It teaches that even the universe must die to be periodically reincarnated in order to continue the cycle of creation. Nuclear holocaust does not frighten a pious Hindu. Indeed, it may be part of karma and his gods' incomprehensible plans.

As he stood on the street corner, Ashley felt uncomfortable and crowded. The streets were jammed with people. They were underfed and clad in ragged clothing, yet most were surprisingly clean. Even the surrounding buildings seemed shoved together. The structures were shabby with tar-patched roofing and faded signs, most written in English as well as Hindi, the national language of India.

The tram pulled up to the curb, and Ashley became part of the human swarm that poured into the bus. The passengers were jostled and shoved, but accepted this as a condition of overpopulation, not a result of intentional rudeness.

Despite efforts to encourage birth control and reduce the burden of too many people, overpopulation remained a major problem in India. Trying to educate masses of largely illiterate poor was a formidable task, but once again, religion was the biggest factor to deal with. Hindus believed that one would shuffle to the next incarnation after death more swiftly if his children prayed for his soul. The more children who prayed for him, the better his odds of a rapid reincarnation. To a Hindu, this is both simple and practical.

Ashley leaned against an open window, desperate for a breath of air that had not been recycled by dozens of other lungs. God, Ashley thought. He wanted to return to England. The London office of Agriculture International had sent Ashley to New Delhi to arrange an education program on advanced farming methods in India. Bloody waste of time. The Americans were already running such a program as part of a foreign-aid policy. The Indian government might be willing to accept London's offer, if they could get everything free.

In Ashley's opinion, the bloody Indian parliament wanted everything handed to it on a silver platter. They expected the governments of the West to look after them like a nation of war orphans, especially the United States and Great Britain. The Yanks were supposed to feel guilty about that nasty gas leak that killed more than a thousand Indians.

Of course, that was nothing compared to the sins of the British Empire. England had established a foothold in India in the seventeenth century, and its influence and power steadily increased during three hundred years of

British rule. The maharajas who ruled the complex monarch states of the past had welcomed the British. But there was no doubt that this imperialist reign was unfair to the people of India in general, though they were probably no better off under the maharajas before the British arrived.

After India gained its independence under Gandhi, the country modeled its constitution on British democracy. English law is still the basis of India's judicial system. Indian schools and military also reveal British influence. The Crown had made some positive contributions to India, but nobody cared to talk about that anymore.

Two more days, Ashley thought. Then he would be on a British Airways flight back home. Thank God. Ashley gazed out the window as the tram rode through the pothole-marred streets. The city of New Delhi looked the same everywhere. Hundreds of Indians, most living in various degrees of poverty, shuffled along the sidewalks. There were a few priests dressed in robes and some blokes wearing turbans. Cows and dogs mingled with the crowds. The damn place was depressing to Ashley. New Delhi made the worst English slum look like Buckingham Palace.

At last the tram stopped at the Royal Suite Hotel, and Ashley gratefully left the bus and entered the building. He got his key from the front desk and headed for the stairs. Damned if he would trust the bleedin' birdcage on a cable that the hotel called an elevator.

The Briton mounted the first two flights of stairs to the third story. Ashley found the door to his room and inserted the key. He unlocked the door, eager for a lukewarm bath and a gin and tonic.

As he entered the room, Ashley caught a fleeting glimpse of something moving behind the door. An object flashed over his head, and the Briton's throat was suddenly trapped by a terrible constriction that encircled his neck. Someone slammed the door as hands grasped Ashley's wrists before he could resist his attackers.

There were three of them, Ashley realized. One held each arm while the third throttled him. The assailants did not give him a chance to defend himself. A foot stamped the back of his knee and threw the Briton off balance. He fell to both knees. His attackers held on and the cord at his throat continued to strangle him.

Edward Ashley was too astonished to be frightened, although he realized death was closing in rapidly. Why were these men killing him? Ashley was just a representative for an agricultural firm, not a politician or an agent for Her Majesty's Secret Service. Why...?

This question was Ashley's last conscious thought. Without ample oxygen to the brain, he blacked out.

The assassins held Ashley to the floor and choked him until they were certain he was dead, then they released their victim. The strangler unwound his weapon from the dead man's neck. He untied a knot in the center of the yellow scarf and removed a silver coin.

"Bhowani," he chanted softly. *"Ma, Durga, Kali."*
"Kali, um kling," the others muttered solemnly.

FRANK KIMBLE'S DREAM had come true. He was an American journalist and photographer who had finally gotten an assignment in India. *Events of the Earth Quarterly* magazine had sent Kimble and his wife, Susan, to cover the Kumbb Mela rites on the Ganges river.

The Kimbles had been delighted to be chosen for this task. It was a once-in-a-lifetime opportunity to visit the birthplace of Asian civilization and witness a spiritual event few Americans would ever get to see. Frank had been fortunate to find a tour guide parked in a Jeep outside the hotel in Calcutta. The guide spoke English and he was quite willing to take the couple to the Ganges for only five American dollars.

"Have you attended the Kumbb Mela before?" Susan asked the guide as he drove the Jeep along a bumpy dirt road.

"No, madam," the guide replied with a smile on his gaunt dark face. "It is not necessary in my religion."

"You're not a Hindu?" Frank inquired.

He hoped the fellow was not a Moslem or a Sikh. Religion is probably the number-one reason for violence in India. Hindus and Moslems get along about as well as the NAACP and the KKK back in the States. And neither the Hindus nor the Moslems had much use for Sikhs—a situation that had become ever more volatile since the assassination of Indira Gandhi.

"There are many forms of Hinduism," the guide replied simply. "Just as the Christians have many different creeds, yet all are Christians. True?"

"True," Frank Kimble agreed, impressed by the simple wisdom of the tour guide. "I understand the Ganges river is very crowded this time of year."

"Almost six million attended last year's ritual," the guide stated. "They flock to the river to bathe in the holy waters of the Ganges. Some believe the Ganges is a goddess of the water. Such foolishness must amuse an educated American like yourself, sahib."

"Of course not," Kimble replied. "I respect the beliefs of others and..."

"I find the Kumbb Mela ritual amusing," the guide said with a laugh. "Did you know that one year more than five hundred people were trampled to death by the other idiots at the Ganges when it was announced that the bathing was to begin? Fanatics killing one another to be the first to splash around in a river. That is insane, is it not?"

"It does seem a bit overzealous," Kimble was forced to admit.

"Senseless death is very sad," the guide said with a sigh as he steered the Jeep toward two men pulling an oxcart. "Killing should serve a purpose."

The guide brought the Jeep to a halt and called to the men with the cart. He stood up as he spoke in rapid Hindi and held the splayed fingers of his right hand at his chest. Kimble did not recall seeing this gesture of greeting used by other Indians before.

"Why are we stopping here?" Susan asked, glancing at the wall of six-foot-high elephant grass that surrounded them. It seemed odd to find such a lonely spot so close to the crowded city of Calcutta.

"I suppose our friend wants to ask these gentlemen about the Kumbb Mela," Frank told his wife. "Maybe he wants to know if anybody has been stomped to death yet."

"That's an awful thing to say, Frank," Susan said with a shiver. "I think something's wrong here..."

"Excuse me, sahib," the guide announced. "These men claim to have found a most ancient relic. It is a good statue of the Jain god Gomatesvara. They are taking it to the city to have it evaluated by experts at the museum. Perhaps you would like to take a photograph of the statue before we continue to the river?"

"You bet," Frank replied eagerly as he climbed from the Jeep.

The two men at the oxcart smiled and bowed at the American. They were dressed only in linen loincloths. Frank was relieved to notice neither man carried a knife. He mentally chided himself for his concern. After all, this was India, not a New York subway where one had to worry about muggers and trigger-happy vigilantes.

He failed to notice the yellow silk scarf that one of the men carried in his fist.

2

Col. Yakov Katzenelenbogen sat at a booth in the Steinberg Delicatessen. The deli claimed to serve the best corned-beef sandwich in Manhattan. Katz had not eaten in every deli in the city, but he was so pleased with the sandwich he was seduced into buying a cheese Danish when he went back to the counter for another cup of tea.

"Only seventy-five cents, and it tastes so good you might faint right on the floor," Edgar Steinberg declared. "But don't do that, please. You might hit your head and hurt yourself."

"Good point," Katz said with a grin as he reached for his wallet.

"You know, a cheese Danish has lots of protein," Steinberg continued. "It's good for you. Quick energy food—"

"Sold," Katz announced, cutting him off.

Edgar Steinberg noticed his customer only used his left hand as he paid for the pastry and he wore a pearl-gray glove on his right. Steinberg also noticed the fingers of his right hand seemed stiff. Probably paralyzed. He guessed the stranger was about fifty-five years old. Probably had a stroke or something.

But Steinberg had a funny feeling about his customer. Katz was a pleasant-looking man. About five ten, a few pounds overweight maybe, but good Jewish food will do that to a fellow, and Steinberg was sure his customer was a Jew. But the guy was not a New Yorker. Nobody is perfect.

Katz's English was precise and proper. Steinberg could not pinpoint Yakov's accent, yet he figured the stranger was originally from Europe.

Perhaps it was Yakov's tweed suit or the fact that he drank tea instead of coffee, but Steinberg decided it was Katz's eyes that convinced him he had guessed correctly. They were expressive blue eyes that revealed humor and sadness, courage and wisdom all at the same time. They were the eyes of a European Jew who had suffered a great deal, but could not be broken. Maybe the inhuman scum that called themselves Nazis had done something to the man's right arm while he was a prisoner in one of their damned concentration camps.

Steinberg was about half right. Katz's parents had been Russian Jews who migrated to France after the Bolshevik Revolution. His father was a superb linguist and translator who raised young Yakov to speak fluent English, Russian, French and German.

The Katzenelenbogen family were victims of Hitler's Holocaust, but Yakov survived. He joined the underground and fought the Nazis. He was later recruited into the American OSS. It was the beginning of a career in espionage, intelligence and covert warfare that would continue for the rest of his life.

After World War II, Katz joined the Haganah in Palestine and fought in the war of independence for the State of Israel. Then there were more wars. He lost his only son and his right arm on a battlefield in the Middle East during the Six Day War. But, Katz continued in his profession and became a top agent in Mossad, Israel's major intelligence and espionage organization.

Katz was perhaps the most experienced espionage operative since the days of Sidney Riley. He worked with the American CIA from time to time and later with the British SIS, the French Sûreté and the West German BND. He had locked horns with the Soviet KGB, ODESSA Nazis and, most of all, international terrorists.

Katz's unique and impressive qualifications had made him the ideal choice to be the unit commander of Phoenix Force, the greatest antiterrorist squad ever assembled.

Katz had not come to the Steinberg Deli to hunt terrorists or enemy agents. He had arranged to meet an old friend, although it would be more than a casual reunion. The Israeli colonel sat at the booth and quietly waited.

At last a short, swarthy man with an iron-gray beard entered the deli. He wore a dark blue pinstripe with a wine-colored tie. The newcomer looked like a Saudi businessman. He was not.

Mohammed Mukdar was a Libyan, a former adviser to Col. Moammar Khaddafi. It might seem odd that such a man would be friends with a former Mossad intelligence officer, but Katz and Mukdar had known each other for many years. They both were opposed to the hatred and prejudice that oppressed the Middle East. Arab and Jew could live in peace if they would only learn to set aside the baggage of the past. Understanding and mutual respect were the only hope for a lasting peace in the Middle East.

Mukdar smiled when he saw Katz. He approached the booth and extended a hand to the Israeli.

"Assa-la'mo alai-kum, kwiyis sa'diq," Katz greeted in Arabic. "Hello, my good friend."

"Shalom, Yakov, chaver," Mukdar replied, repeating the greeting in Hebrew.

"We'd better decide which language to use," Katz suggested as Mukdar slid into the seat across from him.

"Since this is a Jewish restaurant," Mukdar began, "it may be unwise to converse in Arabic."

"I don't think you have to worry about Mr. Steinberg pulling a machine gun from under his counter," Katz assured his friend, but he spoke Hebrew to ease Mukdar's mind.

The only other customers in the Steinberg Deli were a pair of middle-aged housewives who were exchanging stories about how their children made them suffer. One woman had two more offspring than her friend, but the other woman's son had dropped out of medical school so the prize for who had suffered the most remained up for grabs.

"They don't look like an Irgun terrorist hit team," Mukdar commented, tilting his head toward the women. "Besides, it isn't your people I need to worry about."

"Are you certain Khaddafi has sent an assassination unit for you?" Yakov asked grimly, taking a pack of Camel cigarettes from his jacket pocket.

"I'm certain a team of assassins is trying to kill me," Mukdar answered. "I am not certain Khaddafi actually ordered this. As you know, Khaddafi has financed terrorist groups throughout the world, so it is possible one of his 'charity cases' might have decided that killing me would win favor in the eyes of the colonel, who might respond with a generous contribution to repay them for such a favor."

"Right now all that matters is that there's a death threat hanging over your head," Katz said. "Why haven't you gone to the authorities, Mohammed?"

"My dear Yakov," Mukdar sighed. "I fled Libya three years ago and I've never gone to the authorities since. I arrived in the United States with a forged passport, pretending to be an Egyptian tourist. Then I found some people who forged another passport so I could claim I was a refugee from Lebanon. They also forged a green card so I could get employment here."

"But employers usually check on those cards to make certain they're valid," Katz commented as he lit a cigarette.

"I know," Mukdar replied. "But the additional ID helped me move about and find shelter at boarding houses and such. I've been working for people who don't mind hiring illegal immigrants. I've picked lettuce, worked in garment shops and processed chemicals for metal refineries. The work was hard and the wages low by American standards, but I haven't minded it at all. Besides, I haven't had to pay taxes, either."

"Don't tell me you're worried about the IRS," Katz said dryly. "You should have defected directly to the American Embassy in Cairo or Tel Aviv."

"That is exactly what I wish to avoid," Mukdar replied. "I don't want to defect. I'm a Libyan. I still love my country, but I hate politics. I've had enough politics to last a lifetime."

"We've known each other for quite a while, Mohammed," Katz said. "I know that you used to butt heads with Khaddafi when you were his adviser. Not many men would dare criticize his policies against Israel."

"That doesn't mean I approve of everything the State of Israel has done," Mukdar declared.

"That makes two of us," Katz assured him.

"But Khaddafi doesn't believe Israel has a right to exist," Mukdar stated. "He doesn't realize that he's more apt to destroy Libya than Israel. I'm sick to my heart of the politics and bitterness of the Middle East. I am a Moslem Arab and you are a Jew. Does that mean we should be enemies? Is it our duty to hate each other? Both the Koran and the Torah teach that God is mercy and love and forgiveness. Why do so many forget this?"

"People tend to look at religion and take what they want from it and ignore the rest," Katz said with a shrug.

"It's politics," Mukdar insisted. "And I don't want anything to do with it again. I'd rather do honest labor for dishonest employers than work for another government, whether it's Libya or the United States. I am still a Libyan, but I can never go home again. Now all I want is peace."

"Too bad the terrorists stalking you don't feel the same way," Katz said. "What do you want me to do, Mohammed?"

"You're not like me, Yakov," Mukdar began. "You thrive on espionage and intrigue. You were born to be involved in clandestine operations and night raids on enemy bases. You'll never retire from such cloak-and-dagger business."

"So you think I have some sort of covert connection that can help," Yakov said with a smile. "Well, I think I can arrange—"

Suddenly Katz noticed two men at the front door of the deli. They wore dark clothing and black ski masks. The pair were either terrorists or they were fond of winter sports in the middle of July in Manhattan. Katz's left hand quickly slipped inside his suit jacket and drew a SIG-Sauer P-226 pistol from shoulder leather.

"Down!" the Phoenix Force commander shouted as he thumbed off the safety.

The terrorists burst through the door and charged inside, pulling weapons from their coats. One gunman held an Ingram M-11 machine pistol in his fists while the other carried a Colt 1911 A-1 autoloader. Both weapons were equipped with silencers. That meant the terrorists had received some professional training, but Katz did not consider terrorists to be true professionals. Their warped minds and extremist attitudes prevented them from becoming disciplined warriors or competent agents.

But a fanatic amateur can kill you just as dead as an experienced professional.

Katz bolted from his seat, reacting to the situation instinctively. His battle-honed reflexes were faster than his adversaries thought, and Katz immediately evaluated the circumstances and instantly went into action.

He aimed his P-226 at the greater threat—the terrorist armed with the Ingram machine pistol. Katz triggered the SIG-Sauer. A 9mm slug ripped into the terrorist's stomach. Katz had not aimed at the man's chest because the guy held a full-auto weapon that could spray the deli with .380 bullets, threatening the lives of innocent bystanders.

The terrorist doubled up when the 9mm sizzled through flesh and burst the major abdomenal artery. The gunman fired his M-11. Bullets slammed into the floor and buried themselves in the linoleum. The other terrorist swung his Colt pistol toward Yakov, but the Israeli warhorse had dashed to cover at the end of the counter. A .45-caliber missile burned air more than a foot from Katz's new position. The bullet smashed into a cardboard sign advertising hot pastrami and potato salad.

Katz heard the screams of the terrified women. Better frightened than dead, ladies, Yakov thought as he braced the SIG-Sauer across his prosthetic right arm. The Israeli aimed and squeezed off two rapid shots. Both 9mm rounds hit the second terrorist in the chest, left of center. The bullets drilled into the gunman's heart and blasted the life pump apart. The terrorist stumbled, tried to raise his .45 Colt and then crashed to the floor in a lifeless heap.

Two more figures, clad in the ominous nondescript uniform of modern terrorism, burst from the rear door of the deli. Katz had expected this. A two-pronged attack was a professional tactic, but the terrorists did not carry it out in a professional manner. This was typical of their breed. Terrorists usually received only a crash course in weapons, explosives, strategy and guerrilla warfare.

The terrorists did not coordinate their actions to strike simultaneously, and they failed to use distractions to attempt to catch their opponents off guard. Since they didn't care about the lives of innocents, the terrorists could have simply lobbed grenades into the deli, but they chose to come in shooting, probably because they enjoyed seeing the fear on the faces of their victims.

Amateurs, the veteran Israeli commando thought as he shot the closest invader in the face. The terrorist's head recoiled and a red hole appeared at the ski mask between the eyes. An M-11 Ingram slipped from lifeless fingers. The attacker's jacket flapped open as the terrorist fell. Ripe young breasts strained the fabric of the invader's black shirt.

Katz did not mourn the death of the woman killer; female savages can be just as deadly as the males. She had made her own deathbed and now she would lie in it forever.

The terrorist behind the slain female caught her corpse before she could hit the floor. He pushed the woman forward, using her lifeless body as a battering ram. The dead woman struck Katz's arm, jarring the P-226 from his grasp.

"Gotcha, motherfucker!" the terrorist snarled as he aimed a .38 snub-nosed revolver at the Israeli's chest.

Katz raised his right arm and pointed the gloved hand at his opponent. The gunman snickered, amused by the old fool's reaction.

A tongue of orange flame suddenly erupted from the tip of Yakov's index finger, which was actually a hollow steel tube that served as a gun barrel. The terrorist barely glimpsed the flash before a terrible pain lanced through his left eyeball. Blood gushed from the punctured socket as a .22 Magnum round burrowed into the terrorist's brain.

The report of a medium-caliber weapon bellowed within the deli. Katz whirled, his body poised in a crouch. The finger pistol built into the prosthesis attached to the stump of his right arm was a single-shot weapon and there was no time to reload.

Mohammed Mukdar held a snub revolver in his fist, a ribbon of smoke curling from the muzzle. The terrorist Katz had shot in the stomach had started to rise, so Mukdar had shot the man in the back of the head.

Suddenly two more dark shadows with ski masks charged through the front entrance. Mukdar pumped two .38 slugs into the closest attacker. The terrorist, another female barbarian, screamed as bullets punched into her left breast. The woman collapsed, but her male companion fired a Sterling automatic. Mukdar groaned and fell back against the table of the booth.

As the terrorist prepared to put another round in the wounded Libyan, Katz lunged forward and pounced like an angry lion. The Israeli slammed into his opponent. Both men stumbled against the counter, and Katz slashed the side of his right hand across the gunman's wrist. The terrorist cried out in pain as bone snapped. The Sterling autoloader fell from trembling, numb fingers.

Katz swatted the back of his steel hand across the terrorist's face, and the man slid along the glass casing of the counter, blood oozing from his mouth. He spat out two broken teeth and glared at the Israeli pro.

"Sum-bitch!" the terrorist snarled as he swung his left fist at Katz's face.

The Phoenix Force commander raised his right arm and blocked the punch with the metal prosthesis. The terrorist grunted when his forearm connected with steel. Katz slammed his own left hook to the bastard's jaw, knuckles cracking against bone forcibly.

The Israeli swiftly swung a leg and kicked the terrorist in the groin. The steel toe of his shoe smashed into the killer's testicles, mashing them into pulp. The man doubled up with a choking gasp. Then Katz stepped forward and karate-chopped the terrorist at the base of the skull.

The savage fell to his knees. Katz hit him again, using the edge of his steel hand as a club. He struck a third blow to the seventh vertebra in the terrorist's neck. Bone crunched and the assassin dropped face first to the floor—dead.

"My God!" Steinberg exclaimed as he cautiously peered up from behind the counter. "My place looks like a goddamn slaughterhouse!"

"Sorry," Katz replied gruffly, more concerned about his wounded friend than the condition of the delicatessen. "It wasn't my idea."

"Edgar!" one of the women at the opposite end of the room cried out. "I think Sara is dead! God in heaven, those gangsters killed her!"

"I'll call an ambulance," Steinberg announced. "And the police...and my lawyer. Hey, you in the tweed suit who kills people. You a cop or what?"

Katz ignored him. He had placed two fingers to Mukdar's neck, hoping to find a pulse. There was none. The Israeli shook his head sadly and gently pressed Mukdar's eyelids shut.

"Sara is alive!" the woman declared. "She only fainted. Wake up, Sara. You trying to give me a heart attack? I should kill you for scaring me so!"

Yakov Katzenelenbogen found his SIG-Sauer P-226 and returned the pistol to the shoulder holster under his jacket. Then the commander of Phoenix Force folded Mukdar's pudgy hands on his chest.

"Ila al-laqah," Katz whispered, saying goodbye to Mohammed Mukdar for the last time. "May you finally find a lasting peace with Allah in paradise, my friend."

3

"I'm sorry about your friend, Yakov," Hal Brognola said. "But I'm concerned about our security."

Brognola had to worry about security. The cigar-smoking Fed was the head of Stony Man operations. Originally established to combat international terrorism, Stony Man had to maintain strict secrecy because it had formerly been headquarters for a man who was officially dead, a man who had been a fugitive of justice, hunted by the FBI and every police department throughout the United States. That man was Mack Bolan, better known as the Executioner.

Bolan had taken on the Mafia in a one-man crusade that had lasted several bloody years. To everyone's astonishment, especially the Executioner's, he had emerged from the war victorious. The President of the United States had offered Bolan a new life—and a new war against the modern vandal hordes of international terrorism.

A man known as Col. John Phoenix had risen from the ashes of Bolan's past. He and Hal Brognola created Stony Man, an operations base that included the unique squad called Phoenix Force.

Brognola was the go-between for the White House and Stony Man. The Oval Office was the only branch of the United States government that knew anything about

Stony Man, and even the President knew only what Brognola felt he needed to know.

The organization had nearly been scrapped when Mack Bolan became a fugitive once more. The Executioner was now the most wanted man in the world. Every major intelligence and law-enforcement agency in the West as well as the East wanted Bolan—dead or alive. The Executioner was once again a lone wolf pitted against impossible odds. Even Stony Man could not help him now.

However, Stony Man and Phoenix Force continued. It was different without the man who had been the inspiration and central energy of the organization. Gradually the nature of the assignments also changed as terrorism became more sophisticated and dangerous.

Terrorists were often pawns of a greater conspiracy. The KGB, ODESSA Nazis trying to rebuild the Third Reich and others might be the masterminds behind terrorist activity. Phoenix Force had recently clashed with two new international criminal organizations, as well. MERGE was an unholy union of several crime networks—the Mafia, the Corsican syndicate, the Mexican Mafia and the Colombian syndicate. Together, they formed an incredibly powerful and dangerous organization.

TRIO was equally formidable. An Oriental counterpart of MERGE, TRIO consisted of the three great crime networks of Asia—the Black Serpent Tong, the Yakuza Snake Clan and the New Horde, which claimed to be a modern version of the Golden Horde that had conquered most of the world under the leadership of Genghis Khan. The Chinese, Japanese and Mongolian crime masters were as shrewd and ruthless as any Mafia don. The shadow empires of both MERGE and TRIO were growing larger, and the tentacles of these sinister organizations extended across the globe.

The cannibals seemed to be multiplying rapidly. They were becoming bolder, even more ruthless than before, probably because they believed the Executioner was no longer a threat. Perhaps the world was slowly going mad, and this was simply a symptom of international lunacy.

Phoenix Force would do whatever was necessary to combat the madness. They would take on the cannibals anywhere and any way they got the job done. Phoenix expected no quarter and seldom gave any.

"Stony Man is still secure, Hal," Katz began as he sat at the conference table in the Stony Man war room, lighting a cigarette. "Mohammed Mukdar contacted me by telegram. He sent it to the Israeli embassy in Washington, D.C. Mohammed realized I still have connections with Mossad, and he knew I'd receive the telegram eventually. Of course, he used a code name only I would recognize. He was a good man. The world needs more like him."

"Well," Brognola said with a shrug, "everything is squared away with the Manhattan police. They think you're an Interpol agent, Yakov. The cops are gonna take most of the credit, which isn't fair, but it helps us maintain security."

"Any info on the terrorists who attacked Yakov at the deli?" Gary Manning inquired as he sipped black coffee and leaned back in his chair.

Manning was a powerful man, ruggedly handsome and built like a lumberjack from his homeland of Canada. He was one of the best demolitions experts in the world. Manning could handle any kind of explosive with uncanny skill. He was also the best rifle marksman on the Phoenix Force team. Manning had acquired his early combat experience as an "observer" with the 5th Special Forces in Vietnam and later with the GSG-9 antiterrorist squad in West Germany. He was an ideal choice for Phoenix Force. An unflappable professional, he never lost his cool in combat and he tackled every mission with dogged determination.

"Four of the terrorists were Americans," Brognola said, answering Manning's question. "All had been involved in crimes of violence before. Mostly juvenile offenses. One of them had spent a couple of years in the joint for second-degree murder. All four low-lifes had been associated with radical political groups in the past. Interesting variety. The two women were formerly members of something called the Socialist Reform Front. One of the men was a veteran bomb thrower from the old Weathermen outfit of the sixties, and the other guy used to be a member of the National White Supremacy Party."

"Sounds like a fun group," Rafael Encizo said dryly.

Encizo was a native-born Cuban who had been fighting injustice and tyranny since he was a boy in Havana. Most of Encizo's family had been slaughtered by Castro's Communists, and the young Rafael forced to flee to the United States. He had returned to Cuba among the freedom fighters at the Bay of Pigs invasion, where he had been captured and sent to El Principe. Although beaten and tortured, the tough Cuban had escaped from the infamous political prison and returned to the U.S.

He'd had many unusual jobs in America, having worked as a diving instructor, treasure hunter and professional bodyguard. He was a private investigator, specializing in maritime-insurance claims when Stony Man recruited him for Phoenix Force. An excellent frogman, superb knife fighter and an expert at breaking and entering, Encizo was a valuable addition to the special antiterrorist unit.

"The other two terrorists were Syrians," Brognola explained. "Members of the Palestine Rejection Front. You're all familiar with that bunch. One of the dead men was Ali Nassan, believed to have commanded other hit teams in the Middle East and Western Europe."

"The PRF considered Mohammed Mukdar to be a traitor to the Arab people," Katz added. "They may have ordered the assassination of Mukdar without any encouragement from Colonel Khaddafi. We'll probably never know for certain."

"Great motive for murder," Calvin James muttered with disgust. "Mukdar believed Jews and Moslems could live together in peace, so somebody killed him."

James was the youngest member of Phoenix Force. A tall, lanky black man, James was a product of a ghetto in the south side of Chicago. Growing up, he had learned to take care of himself with fists, feet and blade. At the age of seventeen, James had joined the Navy and become a hospital corpsman for the elite SEAL (Sea, Air and Land) tactical unit. He had served his time in the hell known as Vietnam and returned home to continue studying medicine and chemistry on the GI bill.

However, when James's mother and sister had both become victims of crime, the black man decided to join the San Francisco Police Department. He had been a member of the city's SWAT (Special Weapons And Tactics) squad, where he was when Phoenix Force recruited him for a mission more than a year ago. James had been with the unit ever since.

"Murders are often committed for reasons that don't make much sense," Brognola remarked, reaching for a file folder. "In fact, the President of the United States has taken a personal interest in a seris of bizarre killings that have recently occurred in India."

"Does that mean we've got a new assignment?" David McCarter asked eagerly.

The British commando had become restless and started to pace the floor. McCarter was a bundle of nervous energy, and he could never sit still for long. The Briton was a war machine, a former sergeant in the elite Special Air Service. He had seen action in the jungles of Southeast Asia, the mountain range of Oman and the streets of Northern Ireland. McCarter had participated in Operation Nimrod, the famous SAS raid on the Iranian embassy in London. He was an expert pilot who could fly anything from a glider to a 747 and an exceptional pistol marksman. McCarter and Phoenix Force were perfect for each other.

"Yeah," Brognola confirmed. "You guys have a mission. The murders in India haven't gotten much press attention, but a lot of people are getting killed over there and some folks in high places are getting worried about it."

"Like the President of the United States," Encizo mused.

"And the prime minister of Great Britain," the Fed added. "The president of France and the prime minister of the Federal Republic of Germany and a couple other heads of Western democracies are also interested."

"Sounds fascinating," McCarter remarked. "And we haven't heard any details yet."

"Okay," Brognola said as he nodded. "Somebody is murdering Americans, Britons and Western Europeans in India. A few victims have been minor officials working for the embassies in New Delhi. Others have been businessmen and trade representatives. Most were just tourists. The murders have occurred all over the country, from Bombay to Calcutta.''

"How long has this been going on?" Manning asked.

"Almost a year now," Brognola answered. "At first the motive appeared to be robbery. The killers steal their victims' money, watches, rings and so forth, but we don't believe that's the real motive."

"I don't know, Hal," Calvin James said with a shrug. "I've known junkies who would kill people for twenty bucks. That kind of money would mean even more to some poor bastard in a country like India."

"But the murders have all been committed the same way," the Fed explained. "The victims were strangled to death. The murders were well thought out in advance and the killings were done swiftly, skillfully, in an organized manner."

"Or a ritualistic manner," Katz commented thoughtfully. "Does it say if the murders were committed by more than one assailant? Probably two men holding the victim while a third strangled him with a weapon that could be a silk scarf with a silver rupee knotted in the middle?"

"Yeah," Brognola said with surprise. "How did you know?"

"That's the traditional method of assassination by the Thuggees," Katz replied. "Although they'd call it a 'ritual sacrifice,' not murder."

"I've read a bit about the Thugs," McCarter announced. "Cult of robbers who strangled their victims. Thuggee is where we get the English term 'thug,' in fact. As I recall, they were active in the 1840s. We British were occupying India at the time. Our soldiers rounded up the bastards and hanged the lot of them. I thought that was the end of the Thugs."

"Think again," Katz told him. "The British executed hundreds of Thuggees, but they only drove the other members of the cult underground. The religion is still practiced to this day. In fact, there was a revival of the Thuggees in the Bengal region as recently as 1947."

"And the Indian CID thinks that's what's happened now," Brognola confirmed.

"You seem to know all about this cult, Yakov," Encizo remarked. "What else can you tell us?"

"Well," the Israeli began, "they worship the goddess Kali, and according to legend, Kali is the daughter of Shiva, one of the three great gods of the Hindu religion. She is the goddess of death, but also the giver of life and the destroyer of evil."

"This is all very interesting," Encizo remarked. "But I don't see why Stony Man is getting involved in a series of murders committed by a band of religious fanatic *bandidos*. I'd think the Indian CID would handle it, or possibly the CIA and the European intelligence outfits. They already have agents operating in India, don't they?"

"Not as many as you might think," Brognola replied. "The Indian government doesn't seem terribly upset about Americans and Britons being strangled in their country. Apparently none of the victims of the Thuggees have been Indians. They figure it's our problem. The British SIS has to keep its activity in India to a minimum. That's still a sensitive area of the world for the British. Still some hard feelings there."

"I don't know why India is still pissed off at England," McCarter said with a shrug. "British rule ended there some time ago and they haven't done such a great job of running the country on their own."

"France and Germany have virtually no operatives in India," Brognola continued. "And the United States has only a handful of CIA people there. They have to keep a very low profile, especially since Mrs. Gandhi was assassinated."

"Christ," Manning muttered. "Is the Company worried about that stupid accusation the Soviets made about the CIA being involved in Mrs. Gandhi's death? That was such a weak story with absolutely nothing to support it that they didn't even bother to print it for more than a week or so in *Pravda*."

"Some of those theories resurfaced after the chemical disaster at Bhopal," the Fed explained. "The pesticide plant was a Union Carbide installation and the incident was the worst industrial accident in history. Two thousand five hundred killed, thousands more blinded or maimed for life. Can't expect Americans to be very popular in India after that. Of course, the CIA isn't real popular anywhere these days."

"What about the NSA?" Encizo asked Brognola. "Don't they have bases in India?"

Brognola thought for a moment. The National Security Agency was much larger than the Central Intelligence Agency, although most Americans knew virtually nothing about the NSA. The organization was established by executive order during the Truman administration and it has successfully maintained a low profile. The NSA Signal Intelligence probably gathers more covert information than the FBI and CIA put together.

No crusading congressional committees have ever demanded a full-scale investigation of NSA activities. The American media, which has been very alarmed by many practices of other intel organizations, has not expressed much interest in the National Security Agency, although the SIGINT Department conducts surveillance operations within the United States as well as other countries.

"The NSA has an efficient intel network in India," Brognola answered. "But they've been concentrating on the borders along Pakistan and China."

"Certainly the NSA is keeping tabs on the domestic situation in India," Katz remarked.

"Sure," the Fed confirmed. "Especially the turmoil between the Hindus and the Sikhs. But the Thuggees don't seem to be a threat to national security—at least not to the NSA—and it's simply not the sort of thing those sneaky Pete guys are used to handling."

"Maybe you'd better check our records, Hal," Manning said. "Phoenix Force has never gone up against Thuggees, either."

"Yeah," Brognola admitted. "But you guys have tangled with secret societies involved in terrorist activities before. The Black Alchemists were sort of a voodoo cult. The Tigers of Justice were self-styled ninja. And, of course, there was that unauthorized mission you guys carried out in Israel against the Assassins."

"That was my idea," Katz replied. "I'm surprised you're still upset about that, Hal."

"I still have bite marks on my butt from the ass chewing the President gave me," Brognola stated. "But you fellas did find and destroy a very dangerous conspiracy in the Middle East that could have caused World War III."

"I wasn't with Phoenix Force at the time," James said. "But I was told about that mission. Some fanatics had revived the ancient order of the Assassins, right?"

"And what a bunch of bloody lunatics those blokes were," McCarter declared. "They believed their leader was a prophet of Allah. Didn't give a damn if they got killed in the service of their master because they figured they'd go straight to paradise."

"We can expect the Thuggees to be much the same," Katz announced. "You see, some six hundred years ago, the original Assassins network extended across most of Asia, including India. There is evidence to suggest the cult of the Assassins influenced the followers of Kali who then became the 'children of death.'"

"What sort of evidence?" Manning asked with a frown. "The Assassins were Moslems and the Thugs were Hindus. How did one influence the other?"

"Not all Thugs were Hindus," Katz corrected. "Most Thugs came from the Bengal region where Hindus and Moslems have generally gotten along better than they do anywhere else in India. Unfortunately both were known to join the cult of Kali. Also the Thugs used various passwords and key phrases, among them some salutations honoring the Islamic prophet Ali. The Assassins were traditionally products of the Israelis, who regard Ali as the greatest prophet of Allah. This sets them apart from most Moslem sects, including most Indian Moslem sects, who consider Mohammed to be the supreme prophet."

"Well," McCarter said as he fished a pack of Players cigarettes from his jacket. "These Thugs sound like interesting chaps. One thing I can't stand is a dull opponent."

"How many victims have the Thuggees claimed so far, Hal?" Manning inquired.

"Our sources have confirmed fifty-three, but it might be more than that," the Fed replied, checking his notes.

"Twenty-four were British, sixteen Americans and the rest have been French, German, a couple of Italians and at least one Swiss national. He was from a banking interest sent to strike up a deal with the gold market in Bombay."

"Among the victims," Katz asked, "were there any women?"

"I don't think any of them were," Brognola answered, scanning a list of names. "Nope. Not a single woman among the victims. In fact, the killers throttled an American journalist named Frank Kimble right in front of his wife. When she tried to stop them, the Thugs just pushed her aside, but they didn't strike her."

"That's odd," Encizo remarked. "Bandits and terrorists seldom care about the sex of their victims."

"Thuggees would," Katz stated. "They have several taboos in the cult of Kali, one of which is never to take the life of a woman. After all, Kali is a goddess. Sacrificing a female would be sacrilegious."

"Maybe we should dress in drag for this mission," McCarter joked. "Just to be on the safe side."

"David," Katz began with a grin, "if any of us wanted to play it safe, we never would have joined Phoenix Force in the first place."

4

Ranjit Nangal stood on the rock ledge by the mouth of the cave. His long yellow robe hung loosely on his small, scrawny frame. Nangal wore a necklace of small copper skulls and held a pickax with a silver blade. Nangal was a guru, the religious leader of the cult of Kali.

More than two hundred followers had assembled at the foot of the mountain. Most wore ragged clothing. Some were clad only in a dhoti, the garment usually associated with Mahatma Gandhi. A few wore long silk jackets and had yellow turbans bound about their heads. One of these men was Ram Somnoka, a rajput, or son of a maharaja.

The congregation looked to Nangal for enlightenment. The little man was the voice of Kali, the prophet of the great goddess. Nangal addressed the crowd in a reedy voice that echoed within the rock walls of the valley. His voice may have seemed comical to one who failed to realize the power Nangal commanded.

"O loyal children of Kali!" the prophet cried. "The great mother goddess, greater than Lord Shiva who fathered her. For Kali is all things that are woman and all things that are the universe. She is destruction and she is life. She is birth and she is death. She is the pure virgin and the loyal wife."

"Kali bhai, salam," several Thuggees chanted.

"Bhowani, Kali ah-ka-sha," others added.

"It is good that you praise Kali," Nangal declared. "It is good that you honor the goddess of all things. But actions are needed as well as words, my children. Actions and sacrifice. For we are privileged to be her servants, and we have been born at the time of great evil known as *Kaliyuga*. Only *Kalipuja*, the worship and sacrifice to our goddess, can assure us of nirvana when the evil time and our life on this earth have both come to an end."

Nangal waved his silver pickax across the congregation like a magic wand. The followers trembled, for they knew the prophet would now speak of a matter both profound and divine.

"Yet some of you question the word of Kali," Nangal declared. "You hesitate to use the silk scarf that is the instrument we must use to slay the evil ones, the devils who walk like men. For the great Kali is also Durga, the slayer of devils.

"You know the saga of her victories on earth," the guru continued. "Once devils walked the earth and Kali struck them down. The goddess of glory ripped the evil ones to pieces as a lioness would tear a goat asunder. Yet every drop of blood gave seed to a new monster. So Kali had to kill the beasts without shedding their foul blood. And Kali defeated the devils of that day. So it is our duty to sacrifice the evil ones of the present in the manner taught to us by Kali."

The congregation bowed solemnly and began to chant, but Nangal demanded silence.

"Perhaps some of you doubt my word as the high priest of Kali," he declared. "Perhaps you do not understand why Kali wants you to sacrifice the Americans and the Europeans, who are pale-skinned demons the color of a bloodless corpse, yet we are to spare the Russians who have this same color. Kali does not need to justify her law to mortals. If a thing is to be done, it is our duty to do it. If a thing is taboo, it is not our place to ask why."

The congregation uttered a collective murmur. They were obviously dissatisfied with the guru's statement, although none dared openly oppose or criticize Nangal. The prophet once again called for silence.

"However," he began, "Kali understands that doubt is part of human nature. She realizes the weakness of mortal faith, and she shall once again demonstrate the truth of her law. Chopra! Kosti! Bring the infidel and the Russian soldier so all may see the judgment of Kali with their own eyes!"

Four figures emerged from a tent at the base of the mountain. Chopra and Kosti, two lesser priests under the command of Prophet Nangal, escorted two white men from the tent. Chopra was a large man for an Indian, well fed and well muscled. He was a formidable man with heavy eyebrows and a lantern jaw. Chopra's appearance was not deceptive. He was an expert in *vajra-musti* wrestling, and he could kill with his bare hands.

Kosti was barely five feet tall, but his slender body was knotted with muscle. The little Indian smiled constantly, as if forever enjoying some great personal joke. The followers of the cult believed this was because Kosti was filled with the joy of spiritual enlightenment. In truth, Kosti was a deranged sadist who smiled because his twisted mind was usually daydreaming about torture and murder. When he was not thinking about such deeds, he was doing them. Kosti had truly found an occupation he loved.

One of the men accompanied by the two priests was an athletic fellow with dark blond hair. He wore a military uniform with a light blue beret. His unit badge was an enameled white parachute against a blue background with a bright red star. He was a member of the Vozdushno Desantnye Vejska, a Soviet airborne unit. The wide gold band on the shoulder board of his uniform labeled him as a senior sergeant.

The Russian paratrooper proudly marched forward, throwing out his legs in an arrogant goose step. The sergeant did not appear to be afraid of the demonstration that was about to take place.

The fourth man did not share the Russian's attitude. Kosti and Chopra had to shove him forward. His torn white shirt was spotted with crimson and his khaki shorts were soiled. The man's hands were tied behind his back and his mouth was wrapped with white cloth blotched with blood.

"Behold, my children!" Nangal declared. "Before you stands a Russian soldier who is here by choice and not held prisoner. The other is an Englishman. He would try to run from the judgment of Kali, for he knows our goddess is the slayer of evil. When captured, he tried to bite off his own tongue in order to spit blood on the ground to create more British monsters like himself, just like the devils who opposed Kali in the past."

The crowd gasped in amazement at this tale. In fact, the Briton had not bitten his tongue. He no longer had one. Kosti had cut out the man's tongue. That was simply a precaution. A silent man with his hands bound behind his back can only protest accusations by shaking his head.

"Now, my children," Nangal announced. "Behold the goddess Kali!"

An incredible figure appeared at the mouth of the cave. The Thuggees gasped and lowered their heads in prayer. They chanted salutations to Kali and swore their everlasting devotion to the mother goddess.

Seated upon a throne was the goddess Kali. Her face was striped with yellow. The features were fierce: cat eyes and a snarling mouth with purple lips. Her hair jutted with black bristles and green serpents were bound about her head. Kali seemed to glide to the edge of the stone ledge, levitating the throne with her.

The goddess had eight arms, long and serpentine, like the tentacles of a squid. Four of her hands were fisted around the handles of knives. Two other fists held fighting hatchets and a seventh hand clutched the shaft of a lance. The eighth and final hand held a severed human head.

A necklace of yellow skulls hung down to the creature's heavy, full breasts. The figure was bronze and would have appeared to be a statue if it did not move.

But it did move.

The eight arms rose and lowered like a spider in its web. Kali's head moved from side to side, eyes shifting in their metal sockets. Even the severed head in Kali's fist appeared to be alive. Its mouth opened and closed like a puppet and occasionally the disembodied head blinked its eyes.

Kosti and Chopra shoved the Briton into a clearing between the congregation and the tent. The Russian strode forward without encouragement. The crowd moved away from the two priests and the strangers.

"The judgment of Kali is the ultimate truth," Nangal announced. "See that judgment now!"

Kali's necklace of skulls began to glow. Suddenly, a wide beam of light jetted from the skull at the breasts of the goddess. Like a column of hot steel, the blue-white light descended upon the British prisoner.

He did not burst into flame or melt down to a pile of bones. The Briton simply vanished. His body dissolved; flesh, blood and bones were annihilated in the twinkling of an eye. A charred spot on the ground was all that remained of the man.

The crowd was stunned by the awesome display of power by their mighty goddess. They dropped to their knees and lowered their foreheads to the ground. The Russian paratrooper followed their example. The congregation began to chant to Kali, praising her name and asking for the strength and good karma to do her will.

MAJ. MIKHAIL YOUSOPOV sat in a scoop-backed chair as he watched the "goddess Kali" slide backward along an iron rail in the floor. Two Russian technicians moved to the rear of the figure and went to work with screwdrivers. They removed the backplate and examined a maze of circuits and transistors inside Kali.

"Is something wrong with it?" Yousopov frowned. "Everything seemed to work fine during the demonstration."

"*Da*, Comrade Major," one of the technicians replied, glancing up from the statue. "But this was the first time the laser was used. We just want to check to be certain none of the circuits was damaged in the process."

"*O'chen korasho,*" the major replied. "Very good, comrade. You are doing a fine job. Please continue."

Yousopov stuck a black Russian cigarette in his mouth and snapped the flame of a lighter to attention. He glanced about at the generators, computers and control panels that lined the rock walls of the room. It had cost Moscow more than two million rubles to build this complex base inside the mountain of Kali. Some of the best engineers and electronics experts from the U.S.S.R.

had been involved with the project. The major was glad a state-of-the-art air-conditioning unit had been included.

The quarters were certainly more comfortable than those Yousopov had received during his last assignment in Afghanistan. An officer in the Komitet Gosudarstvennoi Bezopasnosti—the Committee for State Security or KGB—Yousopov had been in charge of a network of informers within Afghanistan.

For reasons that Yousopov could not understand, many Afghans objected to the occupation of their country by the Soviet military. Damned rebels were actually attacking Russian troops. They did not appreciate that Moscow was trying to save Afghanistan from the insidious scheming Western imperialists and to bless their nation with the joys of communism under the wise leadership of the Soviet Union.

So Yousopov's spies reported the locations of pockets of Afghan rebels. Then the KGB major reported the information to the Kremlin. The Soviets showed the rebels the error of their ways by spraying them with poison gas and firebombs.

Yet many Afghans still refused to accept that the Russians were in their country for their own good. In fact, an alarming number of Russian soldiers had even defected to join the rebels. They had obviously been brainwashed by the capitalist spies in Afghanistan because they were uttering subversive slogans such as "I don't wish to make war on women and children."

Major Yousopov never worried about abstract notions such as morality or politics. The Soviet Union might not be the "Worker's Paradise" and it was certainly not the center of freedom and equality, but Yousopov was comfortable with his position in the KGB. He had ambitions to rise higher in the ranks of power, so he welcomed his new mission in India.

In Moscow they referred to the operation as "Postcard." The name had no connection with anything the KGB was involved with in India, but one seldom gives a clandestine operation a title that hints of its true nature. Such dramatic nonsense might be all right for espionage in fiction, but it is sloppy security in reality. And no one could afford to get sloppy with Operation Postcard; it was one of the most ambitious schemes the KGB had ever undertaken.

Unfortunately great ambition usually means high risk, and Postcard was no exception. Yousopov realized that success would mean a promotion with honors. Failure would mean a firing squad...if he was lucky. The mission was crazy, but that was one reason it had been successful thus far. Yousopov just hoped his luck would continue to hold for a while longer.

Ranjit Nangal entered the control room. The little guru smiled as he patted Kali's bronze head. Nangal reached inside his robe and extracted a gold-plated cigarette case and headed toward Yousopov.

"Great show today, wasn't it?" Nangal inquired as he slumped into a chair across from the Russian officer. "We made a wonderful impression on the audience, don't you agree?"

"Shouldn't you be with your flock, Nangal?" Yousopov asked dryly.

"Kosti and Chopera are handling services tonight," Nangal explained as he lit a Turkish cigarette. "Simple stuff, really. The followers of Kali chant and chant and call to the goddess all her many names. Eventually they put themselves into a sort of self-induced hypnotic state. The priests start the chants in a steady rhythm with lots of repetition, and I put in some revolving lights in the walls to add to the atmosphere. After a while those idiots go into a deep trance that they consider the inner peace of Kali. It's very amusing to watch them put themselves in that zombielike condition and then hear about all the silly hallucinations they experience, which they regard as religious visions."

"It sounds very entertaining, Nangal," the KGB man said with a shrug. "But I'm not laughing about some of the failures by your Thuggees."

"I wish you wouldn't call them that," Nangal remarked. "You see 'Thuggee' comes from the word *thagna*, which is Hindi for 'deceive.' Thuggees are suppose to be the deceivers, but we know they are really the *deceived*. Correct?"

"Stop being so pompous," Yousopov snapped. "Last week your followers strangled an American journalist to death in front of his wife, but they let her live."

"I've explained that before, Major," Nangal sighed. "The children of Kali don't kill for political purposes. They make sacrifices to their noble goddess and slay devils in human form. It's a righteous calling for the sake of Kali, who is mother, wife and virgin all at the same time. Pretty good trick, eh?"

"I know party officials who are whore, saint and father confessor," Yousopov commented. "Can't you convince the Thuggees that women can be devils when they're Americans or British?"

"Absolutely not," Nangal insisted. "India is not the Soviet Union. Women and men are not equal here. In many ways, women are considered inferior to men, but they still receive special consideration and respect. Go to the worst sections of any city or town in India. You will find women in dire poverty, surrounded by thieves and cutthroats. Yet, even among the poorest Indian women, most wear some gold earrings or a necklace of gold. And no Indian would ever consider robbing them of this gold. It simply isn't done in my country."

"We can't afford to let witnesses to Thuggee killings walk away and report descriptions to the police," the major told him.

"Not many whites look very closely at Indians," Nangal remarked. "I doubt that most of them could tell us apart."

"Don't put too much faith in that," Yousopov told him. "And don't forget that not all Europeans and British are white. The Americans are the worst. They have millions of blacks and Asians. We have many different races in the Soviet Union, too, but we don't let them travel from country to country or let minorities get in a position of authority. Those stupid Americans don't enforce such controls."

"Social controls of ethnic groups," Nangal said. "You know, that's how the caste system got started. The Sanskrit word for caste is *varna*, which means 'color.' The ancient Aryans used to rule over the black aborigines and the dark Dravidians."

"At least your Thuggees don't have any taboos about killing people of different races," the major commented. "Providing they don't lose their nerve like that team last night. They failed to carry out the assassination of that German automobile representative. I thought the Thuggees were suppose to be total fanatics, fearless of death and totally dedicated to serving their holy guru and the goddess Kali."

"They are," Nangal replied. "The team last night did not lose their nerve. While stalking the German in the streets of Calcutta, they encountered a pair of cats fighting in an alley."

"Cats fighting?" The Russian glared at Nangal. "What did that have to do with carrying out an assassination?"

"It was a bad omen," Nangal explained. "The team took it as a sign, a mystical warning that their karma was opposed to carrying out the mission that night. It meant Kali had changed her mind, so the team had to come home instead."

"That is the stupidest thing I've ever heard," Yousopov said with disgust. "Isn't there anything you can do about such foolishness?"

"Major," Nangal replied, "we are able to manipulate and control the followers of Kali because they are religious extremists, ignorant, gullible and superstitious. These qualities make them ideal clay in our skillful hands, thanks to your technology and my charisma. However, these same qualities make the people fearful of shadows and bad omens and strange patterns of tea leaves at the bottom of a cup. We can't do away with their superstitions and still manipulate them."

"I don't like it," Yousopov said grimly. "And I'm not certain I can trust you, Nangal. You're only interested in making money."

"And you're only concerned with serving the glorious goals of the Soviet Union?" Nangal laughed. "You have no personal ambitions? Too bad Karl Marx doesn't have a religious cult of pious stranglers. Then you could run the whole mission without me, Major."

"You seem to forget you owe me your life," the KGB agent snapped. "And you're making quite a fortune for a false guru."

"Which reminds me," Nangal said, still smiling. "You owe me five thousand *tolas* of gold."

"Smuggling that much gold into India isn't easy," Yousopov stated. "Your government has strict laws concerning bringing gold into the country. We must be careful because the Soviet Union is the second largest supplier of gold in the world. The customs officials check every Russian plane with extra care. Isn't it considered treason for an Indian to receive gold from smugglers? I'm surprised you insist on it for payment."

"Russian rubles are virtually worthless outside the Soviet Union," Nangal answered. "So I certainly wouldn't want your currency. It is true that the government once tried to make the possession of imported gold an act of treason, but no one in India would obey such a law. Gold has religious significance here. That makes it more important than the laws of men and more valuable than money. Besides, gold is an international form of currency. I know the value of precious metals has slipped a bit, but a man with five thousand *tolas* of gold will still be very wealthy, regardless of the country he chooses to live in."

"Do you plan to leave India, Nangal?" Yousopov asked, raising an eyebrow with suspicion.

"Not for a while," the Indian assured him. "But after this mission is over, I may decide to seek a new residence. Living under Soviet Communism doesn't appeal to me."

"You really are a mercenary," Yousopov said with contempt. "And a capitalist."

"I'm glad we've finally begun to understand each other, Major," Nangal said with amusement.

5

"Who the hell are you people?" Waldo Lampert demanded.

He pointed a gold-plated Cross pen at the five men of Phoenix Force. Lampert was a small, chubby man with a balding head and a round face. He wore horn-rimmed glasses with thick lenses. Waldo Lampert looked like an accountant or a CPA tax man. He blended into crowds like a wrinkled pair of slacks, a useful trait for clandestine operations.

Waldo Lampert was a case officer for the National Security Agency and had been stationed in India since 1976. Like most NSA agents, he regarded the CIA with contempt. Rivalry between intelligence organizations is common throughout the world. Some departments are more concerned about keeping secrets from their own side than from their enemies. Naturally, Lampert assumed Phoenix Force was CIA.

Of course, they did not call themselves Phoenix Force and all five men used cover names and forged ID. Lampert had met them at the airport and driven the team to the Hariana Regent Hotel in New Delhi. The NSA man had barely uttered a dozen words before he and Phoenix Force met with Colonel Sangh in the Regent conference room. Then Waldo Lampert erupted with righteous outrage.

"All I was told was how to recognize you five and bring you here when you arrived," Lampert continued. "I was given no explanation. No information about who you are or who you work for...."

"Are you familiar with the term 'need to know'?" Yakov Katzenelenbogen inquired, scratching his nose with the steel hook attached to his prosthesis. "You've been told what you need to know. When you need to know more, we'll tell you."

"I'm sure you were also told to cooperate with us, Waldo," Rafael Encizo added as he and McCarter began to pry nails from the wooden frame of a crate.

"Don't call me Waldo," Lampert snapped. "You five guys are CIA, dammit."

"Please, Mr. Lampert," Lieut. Col. Bahadur Sangh began. "Let us be civil to our guests, please."

Colonel Sangh was the executive officer of the Indian Criminal Investigation Department. The sad-faced Hindu was clearly distressed by his self-appointed role as peacemaker. If these foreigners wanted to argue, why did they have to come to his country to quarrel?

"Civil?" Lampert glared at Sangh. "These Langley hotshots arrived with that crateful of 'farm machinery.' They had arranged for the NSA to pull some strings so they could avoid customs. Do you know why, Colonel Sangh?"

"I imagine they have some equipment that is confidential for some reason," Sangh replied. "Perhaps radios or computers...."

"For crissake," Lampert groaned. "NSA could supply them with that sort of gear. That crate is full of guns. Correct?"

"Well," Gary Manning remarked, "we also packed some ammunition and explosives. As well as some grenades and a few other tools of the trade."

"This seems rather extreme," Sangh said with a frown. "I realize you five have received special permits to carry firearms while in India, but I assumed this meant permission to carry a pistol for self-defense."

"We just like to be able to defend ourselves against anything that might occur during a mission," Calvin James stated. "Like a full-scale invasion from Pakistan, for example."

"I'm afraid I can't permit you five to go about with an arsenal..." Sangh began.

"Haven't you also been ordered to cooperate with us, Colonel?" Katz asked. "I believe your orders come directly from the office of the prime minister of India."

"Yes," Sangh admitted. "That is true, but I'm not certain the PM fully understands this situation. He is still quite new to his office and preoccupied with many important national concerns."

"Fifty-three murders with the same MO committed all over the country within less than a year isn't considered important?" James raised his eyebrows. "That kind of attitude could ruin your tourist trade, fella."

"I doubt that many Americans were terribly concerned when thousands of Indians were victims of the Union Carbide disaster," Sangh said dryly. "But now that your people are victims, it is a different matter."

"An accident," Manning responded, "even an accident as terrible as that one, is not premeditated murder."

"Right," Lampert agreed. "A series of murders have been committed by some fanatics belonging to a religious cult."

"Thuggees," Katz stated.

"Okay," the NSA man agreed with a nod. "So you figured out that much. Well, things like this happen from time to time in India. Colonel Sangh and the CID are trying to track down the killers right now. What makes you CIA cowboys think you can do a better job than he can? You guys should go back to the States and look into some of the senseless homicides committed back *there*. I keep up with the news about what's going on in America. Fellas crack up and go into fast-food restaurants to shoot down innocent bystanders. Crazies drive from state to state and murder total strangers. A guy in Texas supposedly killed more than three hundred people. Compare that to the fifty-three murders you guys are talking about."

"The murders committed in India aren't the work of a roving serial killer," Encizo told him. "It's a conspiracy to kill Americans, Britons and Western Europeans—citizens of countries that happen to be our NATO allies."

"And you do not regard India as an ally?" Sangh said, frowning.

"Beginning to wonder about that," McCarter said dryly.

"This theory about a conspiracy is a presumption with no proof to back it up," Lampert snorted. "Typical CIA paranoia."

"What makes you so high and mighty?" McCarter asked sharply. "You think you know everything, but you just don't give a damn about the lives of those people who were strangled to death simply because of their nationality."

"It's a police matter," Lampert insisted. "Let Colonel Sangh do his job and keep out of his way. You five don't know India. I'll wager that none of you speak

Hindi or Urdu. You probably don't even know the difference between the two languages.''

"The spoken languages are very similar," Katz, the Phoenix Force linguist, announced. "But Hindi is derived from Sanskrit, so it is written in Devanagari script, left to right—the same as English and European languages. Urdu is written from right to left, the same as Hebrew and most Asian languages. It resembles Arabic script, and it is largely used by the Islamic population in India."

"Big deal," Lampert growled. "But you don't speak either language, do you? How about Punjabi? Malayalam? Kashmiri? There are more than forty languages spoken in India. Do you speak any of them, fella?"

"Do you?" Calvin James asked.

"I manage," the NSA man replied.

"This has gone far enough," Katz declared. "We don't want to pull rank on you fellows, but I'm afraid we have to."

"What?" Lampert scoffed. "I'm NSA. You can't pull rank on me!"

"Check with your control officer and ask him what our authority is," Katz told him. "You'll learn that we are acting on direct orders from the President of the United States. If you refuse to cooperate with us, you'll be replaced by someone else and probably find yourself being debriefed so the National Security Agency can kick you out of their organization."

"You can't..." Lampert began.

"Yes, we can," Manning informed him. "In fact, we could put a bullet through your head and write in our report that you had been killed by a large hailstone. Nobody would ever question our claim, and no one would ever investigate your death."

"This sort of talk is most unseemly," Colonel Sangh declared. "I wish to remind you that this is India, not the United States. You are *all* guests in my country."

"You're wrong, Colonel," Katz stated. "We were not invited to your country, we were assigned to a mission here. Without your cooperation we can't carry out our mission. If that happens, you and your government will regret it. Because if we go home empty-handed, the President will know why we couldn't complete our job here. Then next year's American foreign aid to India will be cut."

Sangh stared at Katz. "You can't be serious."

"The President is the head of the executive branch of the American federal government," Encizo told him. "That means the man in the Oval Office can cut foreign aid or at least tie up delivery for about a year by slugging it out in Congress, which is our legislative branch. The judicial branch doesn't get involved in foreign-aid policies, so don't hope for any help from them."

"I wouldn't count on too many congressmen making an issue of cutting aid to India," James added. "Folks back home are getting pissed off about seeing more tax dollars spent on aid to foreign countries than on social programs in the States."

"Colonel Sangh," Katz continued, "we have no desire to make things difficult for you or Mr. Lampert. All of us are on the same side."

"I'm not so sure about that," Lampert muttered.

"Yeah," James commented. "I know what you mean."

"Gentlemen," Katz said wearily, "we have a mission to carry out. Frankly, if we have to blackmail you two in order to get your cooperation, we'll do it. The mission comes first. If we have to destroy your careers or hit India in the pocketbook, we'll do that, too."

"My God," Lampert whispered. "You really are serious."

"Very serious," the Israeli confirmed. "I would rather every man in this room, including my colleagues and myself, die carrying out our mission than utterly fail to accomplish it."

"I wonder," Sangh remarked, "if you gentlemen are this ruthless toward your allies, how do you treat your enemies?"

"Are you familiar with the passive resistance tactics of Mahatma Gandhi?" McCarter inquired as he lit a Players cigarette.

"Of course," Sangh replied, surprised by the question.

"Well," McCarter said with a chuckle, "we don't use those methods."

"Colonel Sangh," Katz said gently. He knew it was time to mend some fences if Phoenix Force was to get decent cooperation from the NSA and the Indian CID. Yakov did not want his allies to feel any more resentment than they already felt toward the Stony Man commando team. "We don't mean to threaten or intimidate you. Or you, Mr. Lampert. We really don't. You two were chosen to work with us because you're professionals, highly respected in your field."

"Oh, God," McCarter muttered with disgust.

Katz moved forward and managed to step on McCarter's foot without being too obvious. The Briton grunted sourly, but he realized it was time to shut up and let Yakov do the talking.

"Now," the Israeli continued, "you gentlemen are correct. We're not familiar with India and none of us speak Hindi or Urdu. We need your help, but we don't expect you to drop other matters that may very well be more important to international safety and freedom than our mission. I don't know what you gentlemen might have on your plate right now, and I realize I'm certainly not in a need-to-know position concerning India's national security or the NSA operations in this region."

"We have to maintain top-level security about our intelligence gathering," Lampert replied proudly, unaware that Katz was humbling himself to stroke the NSA man's ego.

"Well, your SIGINT has certainly been better at gathering information and keeping secrets than anyone else in the intelligence community," Katz commented with an envious sigh. "That's why we hope you can help us with some information...without jeopardizing any of your sources, of course."

"We'll see what we can do," Lampert said.

"And what do you wish of the CID, Mr. Jacobs?" Sangh asked, addressing Katz by his cover name.

"We need at least one guide and a translator," Yakov explained. "If you can spare more manpower, that would be even better."

"Where do you intend to start?" Lampert asked.

"The most recent murders by the Thuggees were committed about a week ago," Katz replied. "One in Calcutta and the other here in New Delhi. Checking out the scene of a crime seems a logical place to begin an investigation."

"But CID has already investigated those sites," Sangh stated. "I'm afraid the killers left no clues."

"Sometimes a lack of evidence can be a clue," Katz replied.

Sangh and Lampert nodded in agreement because they did not want to admit they did not know what the hell Yakov meant. The CID colonel cleared his throat.

"You'll have the help you need," he announced.

6

Yakov Katzenelenbogen and David McCarter sat in the back seat of the battered old sedan that crept through the streets of New Delhi. Crowds parted to make room for the car. Indians stared at the vehicle with amazement. Automobiles are not common in India. Spectators emerged from shops and markets to get a better look at the mechanical wonder. Trams and taxicabs did not attract such attention, but a private vehicle probably meant the occupants were either government officials or wealthy.

Beggers lined up and extended open palms as they cried for alms. Peddlers waved merchandise and shouted prices. They were remarkably well versed in languages, repeating the offers in English, French, German and Italian. The driver angrily shouted back at the peddlers and beggers in Hindi, pumping the heel of his palm into the horn.

"I apologize for my countrymen," Sgt. Bara Din told his passengers. "They do not understand urgent business."

"They seem pretty urgent to make a profit," McCarter commented, opening a briefcase to check the contents within.

The Briton carried an M-10 Ingram. The compact 9mm machine pistol was one of McCarter's favorite weapons. He also carried a 9mm Browning Hi-Power autoloading pistol in a shoulder rig under his left arm, concealed by a loose-fitting khaki bush jacket.

Katz had the SIG-Sauer P-226 in shoulder leather beneath a linen sports jacket. The Israeli still wore the prosthesis with the three steel hooks. It was more versatile than the five-fingered steel hand. It didn't have a built-in .22 pistol, but the hooks had most of the same functions as flesh-and-blood fingers. The steel talons could also be a formidable weapon at close quarters.

Sergeant Din honked the horn to convince a pair of scrawny cows to get out of the way. The animals sluggishly moved and the CID agent drove on to the Royal Suite Hotel, where Edward Ashley had been murdered.

The hotel desk clerk spoke English, so Katz and McCarter questioned him while Din spoke to some of the servants on the hotel payroll. The clerk had little to say about Ashley's death. He had been quite astonished when the Briton was murdered. As far as he knew, Ashley had no enemies in India and did not appear to be in possession of anything valuable enough to kill for.

"Of course," the clerk said with a sigh, "India is a poor country and some evil persons would consider life of little value. Whoever killed him must have done so simply to claim his wallet and watch. The police told me these things had been stolen."

"No one heard anything suspicious or noticed any strangers lurking about?" Katz inquired.

"I'm afraid not, sir," the desk clerk answered. "It is most unfortunate, but these things happen everywhere. I understand there are so many thieves and killers in America that they have different categories of criminals. Muggers, mass murderers and something called a birdwalker."

"Jaywalker," McCarter corrected. "Dreadful crime, but what can you expect from Americans."

"Very bad people with nuclear bombs and such," the clerk agreed. "And their chemicals killed many Indians, you know."

"Of course, the Yanks have given India tons of food and billions of dollars," McCarter said with a shrug. "But that's all materialistic rubbish."

"Yes indeed." The clerk nodded. "At least they tip well."

"Well," Katz added, "nobody's all bad."

"Gentlemen," Sergeant Din began as he approached the Phoenix Force pair. "I spoke with a bellman who told me the late Mr. Ashley was rather fond of a certain tavern of unpleasant reputation. He went there often. The bellman thinks perhaps Mr. Ashley was doing some business with a notorious Sikh opium dealer known as Abdul."

"Opium?" McCarter frowned. "That doesn't fit the personality profile we read about Ashley."

"Maybe there were some details about Mr. Ashley that he managed to keep secret," Katz commented. "Or perhaps this is just a nasty rumor being spread by a Hindu or Moslem employee who hates Sikhs."

"If I may say what I think," Sergeant Din said, "we should check on this tavern. It is called the Peacock's Plume. I have heard of it before. A most unsavory place."

"Well," Katz said, "the Peacock's Plume appears to be the only lead we're going to find here."

"Besides," McCarter added, "we do rather well in unsavory places."

"Speak for yourself," Katz muttered.

Sergeant Din knew the location of the Peacock's Plume. The tavern was a grim little building sandwiched between a curio shop and a dentist's office. A legend above the tavern displayed a faded blue-and-yellow peacock with the name of the establishment written in Urdu and English. The windows were tinted dark yellow.

"These fellows may not speak Hindi," Katz remarked.

"Is no problem, sahib," Din assured him. "I speak Urdu and some Punjabi, as well."

"This place probably caters to Moslems and Sikhs," McCarter commented. "They may not welcome a Hindu, Sergeant."

"Then I simply won't tell them what my religion is," Din said, smiling. "I don't know if you gentlemen are familiar with Islamic taverns. Don't order any drinks with alcohol. Most of these places only serve coffee or tea, although some Moslems will have some whiskey on hand for foreigners."

"We'll bear that in mind," Katz assured him.

"Watch yourselves when we get inside," Din warned. "Some of these taverns can be a bit rough, especially if Abdul is connected with the opium trade."

"Seems reasonable," McCarter agreed. "Let's find out about these chaps firsthand."

They parked the car and walked to the tavern. The door was locked. Din knocked twice, then rapped his knuckles on the door once more. It opened and a tall bearded man with a turban bound around his head appeared. Din spoke to the man and placed an index finger to his teeth. The barman, who appeared to be a Sikh, nodded and tugged at his ear with thumb and forefinger. He looked at Katz and McCarter, a smile barely visible amid his thick black beard.

"Welcome," he greeted. "My name is Abdul. Please, come in."

They entered the Peacock's Plume. The tavern was drab, with a bare wooden floor and crudely designed furniture. There were three tables and a few chairs that were held together with wire wound around their legs. The bar was a plain wooden counter with tin cans of different coffee and tea blends displayed on the shelves. The aroma of freshly brewed coffee filled the room.

Five patrons sat in the tavern. Three men sat at one table, solemnly sipping steaming liquid from china cups. They wore turbans similar to Abdul's headgear. Katz guessed the trio were also Sikhs. The other two customers, seated at a separate table, were clad in dhotis. They were almost certainly Hindus. Whatever sins the Peacock's Plume might be guilty of, discrimination was not one of them.

"Sergeant Din tells me you gentlemen are here to ask me about an Englishman who was recently killed at the Royal Suite Hotel," Abdul began, strolling to the bar. "I heard about the incident. Terrible. He was strangled, correct?"

"That's right," Katz confirmed as he approached the Sikh. "What can you tell us about Mr. Ashley?"

"I'm afraid I do not know this name," Abdul said as he turned toward Din. "Did you tell them that I knew this unfortunate Englishman, Sergeant?"

"That is what I was told," Din replied, holding splayed fingers of one hand to his chest. "A bellman at the hotel..."

"Din est un ennemi," Katz told McCarter, speaking French because the British ace understood the language and the Indians probably did not. "Din is an enemy."

"Merde, alors," McCarter said with surprise.

"They plan to kill us," Katz added as he drew the SIG-Sauer pistol from shoulder leather.

Abdul lunged for Katz's pistol. The Israeli slashed with his prosthetic arm, clubbing the steel limb across the Sikh's chest. The blow knocked Abdul backward into the bar while the two Hindus at the closest table suddenly jumped to their feet. Both men held yellow silk scarfs knotted in the middle. The Thuggees advanced.

Katz promptly shot the closest attacker, pumping a 115-grain hollowpoint into the Hindu's chest. The man cried out and tumbled into the table. He slid across the top and struck a chair. Man and furniture crashed to the floor. Neither moved.

A long wooden pole suddenly lashed out. It connected with Katz's left forearm, jarring the ulnar nerve and forcing him to drop the P-226 blaster. A Sikh from the other table had attacked Katz with a *lathi* stick. A bamboo fighting staff five feet long, the *lathi* is a lethal weapon in the hands of an expert, and Katz did not assume his opponent was a novice.

The *lathi* swung toward Yakov's face. He blocked the attack with his prosthesis and swiftly grabbed the stick with his left hand. The Israeli held on to the bamboo staff as he whirled along the length of the *lathi* to slash the steel claws of his prosthesis into his opponent's turban-covered head. The Sikh groaned and stumbled off balance. Katz quickly yanked the *lathi* from the man's weakened grasp and rammed an end of the stick into his aggressor's solar plexus. The Sikh uttered a breathless gasp and crumpled to the floor.

David McCarter had also drawn his pistol. Sergeant Din had backed away from the Briton and held up his empty hands in surrender. However, the other two Sikhs at the table launched themselves at McCarter, Thuggee strangling cords in their fists.

The British combat pro pivoted and fired his Browning. A 9mm parabellum round smashed into a Sikh's face, cutting through the bridge of his nose to gouge a lethal tunnel in the Thuggee's brain. The Sikh collapsed, but his fanatic comrade kept coming.

Without warning, Din seized McCarter from behind. He grabbed the Briton's bush jacket and yanked it forcibly, pulling it from his shoulders to bind his arms at the elbows. It was an old police-constable trick, and McCarter instantly responded by dropping to one knee and leaning forward. Sergeant Din was thrown off balance and tumbled over McCarter's arched back.

The other scarf-wielding Sikh closed in fast and kicked the Browning from the Briton's hand. As the Thuggee tried to swing the silk loop of his scarf around McCarter's head, the Phoenix pro raised his left arm and blocked the attack with his briefcase. The Thuggee's fists struck leather as McCarter shot upright and shoved hard. The Sikh hurtled backward and toppled into a table.

Din picked himself up from the floor and grabbed a chair. He raised the flimsy furniture overhead and attacked McCarter. The Briton did not have time to retrieve his Browning or take the Ingram machine pistol from its case. He raised the valise to block the chair. The force of the blow tore the case away from the handle, but McCarter was protected from the assault.

The valise fell to the floor as McCarter stepped to the side of his opponent, the handle of the case still in his fist.

The Briton lashed a boot to Din's abdomen, kicking the Indian under the right rib cage before Din could swing the chair again. Din doubled up with an agonized groan.

McCarter chopped the side of his hand across the back of Din's neck and the CID sergeant fell to one knee, trying to break his fall with his hands. Suddenly McCarter grabbed Din by the collar and the back of his belt. The Briton darted to the bar and shoved his opponent, ramming Din's head into the base of the counter. The Indian's body slumped lifeless to the floor, blood and gray bubbles oozing from his skull.

The Briton caught a blur of movement out of the corner of an eye and ducked as a Sikh Thug tried to wrap his scarf garrote around McCarter's neck. The killer pulled hard, startled to find the knotted cloth had caught nothing but air.

McCarter quickly drove a shoulder into his assailant's midsection and grabbed the man's legs. He straightened his knees for leverage and scooped up the distressed Thuggee. Using his shoulder as a fulcrum, McCarter stood and hurled the Sikh head over heels. The strangler screamed as his spine smashed into the edge of the bar. The fifth lumbar vertebra cracked, and the Thuggee slumped over the counter and fell to the floor, his back broken.

Abdul and the last Hindu Thuggee were trying to launch a fresh attack on Yakov Katzenelenbogen. The Israeli warrior still held the *lathi* stick, using his left hand for an anchor and holding the shaft between the hooks of his prosthesis. Abdul appeared to be armed only with his musclar physique, and the Hindu still held his silk garrote. The killers charged, hoping to catch Katz off balance with a two-pronged attack.

The Israeli feinted a roundhouse stroke with the *lathi*. The Hindu held up his fists, forming a silk bar with the taut scarf to try to protect his head. Katz immediately altered his tactics and thrust the *lathi* like a cue stick. The bamboo tip caught the Hindu under the jaw and stabbed the center of his throat. The Thuggee's windpipe collapsed and he dropped his strangler's scarf and stumbled backward, both hands clamped around his crushed throat. The man's mouth opened; spilling crimson drool across his chest. Then he wilted to the floor, dead.

Abdul did not care to take on Katz hand to hand. He suddenly scooped up a table and hurled it at the Phoenix Force commander. Katz tried to block the flying furniture with the *lathi*, but he was not accustomed to the bamboo staff and his prosthesis was clumsy with the unfamiliar weapon. He managed to prevent the table from delivering a crippling blow, but the impact knocked him off balance. Katz fell on his back, still clutching the *lathi*.

With a roar of victory, Abdul charged, determined to crush the Israeli. Katz quickly thrust the *lathi* between his attacker's legs and whipped the stick upward. Abdul's battle cry became a high-pitched shriek as his testicles burst open from the ruthless tactic. He doubled up in agony.

David McCarter moved behind the Sikh and clasped both hands together. He swung a powerful blow between Abdul's shoulder blades. Abdul groaned and fell forward to receive a bamboo swat in the face as Katz lashed out with the *lathi*. As the Sikh fell on all fours, McCarter seized the man's hair and yanked his head back to slam a knee under Abdul's jawbone. The Sikh sprawled on his back, unconscious.

"Are you all right, Yakov?" McCarter asked. He did not offer to help Katz to his feet. The one-armed Israeli would have been offended.

"I'm fine," Yakov assured him. "Didn't take us too long to find some Thuggees, did it?"

"Didn't take them too long to find us, either," the Briton mused. "How the hell did you know it was a trap and Din was in league with the Thugs?"

"I did a bit of research on the Thuggees," Katz explained. "They used a series of secret hand signals. I was suspicious of Din when he knocked on the door by rapping twice and then a delayed third knock. Sounded like a code signal. Then I recognized a number of hand signals used by both Din and Abdul. When Din held his hand to his chest with his fingers splayed—the signal to kill—I figured there was no room for further doubt."

"Sure glad you did," McCarter told him as he retrieved his Browning Hi-Power. "I don't think Colonel Sangh will be very pleased to find out one of his men was an agent for the Thugs."

"Hard to get good help these days," Katz said with a shrug.

7

"I still find this so very hard to believe," Colonel Sangh said, shaking his head with dismay. "How could Sergeant Din be a Thuggee? We checked his background most carefully before accepting him into the Criminal Investigation Department."

"No personnel checks are fail proof," Katz replied as he slumped into a chair beside the CID colonel's desk. "Double agents slip into every intelligence department and you're always going to get a few paranoids, psychopaths and secret fanatics. This is an odd business and it attracts an odd breed of people. After all, the best people for intelligence work are individuals who are good at keeping secrets. It isn't surprising they manage to keep a few things secret about themselves, as well."

"This is terrible," Sangh said, literally wringing his hands like a spinster waiting for the telephone to ring. "I'm no longer certain I can trust the people in my own department."

"Colonel," Katz said, "if you want to trust people, intelligence is the wrong line of work. You must be suspicious of virtually everyone, including people on your side or in your organization. They're in a position to cause you the most harm."

"Well," Sangh said with a sigh, "I certainly wouldn't blame you if you didn't trust us now."

"Whatever gave you the idea we trusted you to begin with?" David McCarter replied as he paced the floor of Sangh's office like a caged lion.

The local police had arrived at the Peacock's Plume a few minutes after the battle with the Thuggees had ended. One of the cops spoke English, and he agreed to let Katz call CID headquarters. When Sangh and his men showed up, the police happily relinquished the case to the CID. Cops throughout the world have one common trait—they do not want to get involved in a political incident.

After tearing the tavern apart looking for clues, the CID cuffed the two surviving Thugs and took them to headquarters. Katz and McCarter rode in Sangh's limousine. The CID colonel seemed terribly embarrassed by the incident. The conversation with the Phoenix Force pair in his office did nothing to ease Sangh's distressed attitude.

"Please don't take offense, Colonel," Katz urged, once again trying to help the CID officer save face. "But we have to be suspicious. We've had missions jeopardized by double agents before."

"I just never imagined such things happening within my organization," Sangh admitted.

"Which is exactly why you were vulnerable to infiltration," McCarter growled. "I just hope the blokes you assigned as guides and translators to assist the other members of our team don't turn out to be Thuggees, as well."

Gary Manning, Rafael Encizo and Calvin James had flown to Calcutta to investigate the murder of Frank Kimble. Two CID agents had accompanied the larger Phoenix Force group to Calcutta. Both men were bilingual, speaking Hindi and English. Lieutenant Tagore was also a helicopter pilot, and Sgt. Sar Ray was born and raised in the Bengal region. Katz found little comfort in this information since the Thuggees traditionally recruited most of their members from Bengal.

The telephone on Sangh's desk rang and the colonel hastily answered it. He smiled with relief when he recognized the voice of Lieutenant Tagore.

"The other members of your team are in Calcutta," Sangh told Katz. "Should I tell the lieutenant to put one of your men on the phone so you may speak with him, Mr. Jacobs?"

"Please," Katz replied.

Sangh handed the phone to the Israeli.

"Jacobs here," Yakov said into the mouthpiece.

"This is Saunders," Gary Manning's voice announced, using his cover name. "We haven't had much luck here. Nobody knows anything about Kimble's death that hasn't already been reported to the police. The most detailed information was Susan Kimble's report to the cops, and it wasn't worth a damn. She described the assassins as 'Indians.' Lot of help that is. The police found the Jeep that the phony guide had used to set up the Kimbles for ambush. The vehicle had been stolen a couple of days earlier from a legit tour-guide service. Whoever stole it had enough sense to paint the Jeep a different color, change the license plates and wipe off fingerprints."

"Apparently the Thuggees have learned to appreciate a few changes since the 1840s," Katz commented. "I don't like talking freely on an open telephone line, but we've had an incident here. Our CID guide led us right into an ambush."

"Jesus," Manning rasped. "Didn't take long for—"

"If the CID men with your group are within hearing," Katz said sharply, "be careful what you say. Either one or both of them could be Thugs. For that matter, this line could be tapped. Better get back to New Delhi. I don't like us being separated like this when the enemy is stalking us. Divide and conquer is not just a slogan, it's good strategy."

"Okay," the Canadian said. "We'll head back pronto."

"Be careful," Katz warned. "And make certain you check the helicopter for booby traps."

"Right," Manning confirmed. "See you in New Delhi."

Katz returned the receiver to its cradle.

"Really, Mr. Jacobs," Colonel Sangh said wearily, "don't you think it's a bit excessive to talk about the phones being tapped? After all, we're dealing with a religious cult, not an international spy ring."

"We can't be entirely sure what we're dealing with just yet," Katz replied. "But we certainly can't underestimate the Thugs. They've managed to carry out fifty-three murders without being apprehended by the police or the CID. They managed to slip at least one agent into your organization who wasn't detected until today. Cult or not, they function like an intelligence network, and we'd better regard them as such."

"Good point," McCarter agreed. "But you realize those blokes in the Peacock's Plume didn't use guns. They even managed to disarm us, and none of them even tried to pick up our pistols. Might have killed us if they had."

"A sacrifice to Kali has to be without shedding blood," the Israeli explained. "I told you about the legend."

"Right," the Briton replied. "They have to kill with a yellow scarf. But you warned Saunders to check for booby traps in the helicopter. Blowing a chap to bits isn't exactly bloodless. Doesn't fit the Thug MO."

"No, it doesn't," Katz agreed. "But at the risk of repeating myself, we don't know enough about our enemies to try to second-guess them. In the past the Thuggees have killed other Indians as well as foreigners. This time, it appears the cult has been selecting only outsiders from the West."

"That could be because the Thugs revival may have been prompted by the Union Carbide disaster," McCarter mused. "It would obviously incite some strong anti-American sentiments. The followers of Kali might decide the Yanks are devils such as those mentioned in the legend."

"That wouldn't explain why they're killing Europeans and Britons," Colonel Sangh commented.

"Resentment against the British is hardly new in India," McCarter replied. "As long as the Thugs are hunting down devils, why not include the English devils of the past? You chaps haven't gotten along too well with the French, either—of course, nobody else does. The Thugs might have added them to the list. The other Europeans who were victims might have been mistaken for another nationality."

"That's possible," Yakov admitted. "But there could be more to this."

"You mean somebody is pulling the Thugs's strings for another reason?" the British ace remarked. "Well, it wouldn't be the first time something like this happened."

"If you'll forgive me for saying this," Sangh began, "you two are jumping to conclusions."

"We're not reaching any conclusions just yet," Katz corrected. "But we are considering some possibilities. Perhaps you could do us a favor, Colonel."

"A favor?" Sangh said with a sigh, aware that he had little choice about obeying any "request" Phoenix Force might make. "What is it, Mr. Jacobs?"

"Please find out the locations of temples and worship halls dedicated to the godddess Bhowani," Katz said. "I doubt that any Thuggees would openly worship Kali, but the goddess is also known under several other names that aren't usually connected to the cult of stranglers."

"I'll see what my people can come up with," Sangh answered. "But there are probably hundreds of such temples scattered throughout India and none of them are necessarily connected with the Thuggees."

"I realize that," Katz confirmed. "But have your people do a computer check for anything that may have been reported as unusual activity at any of these temples. Traditionally, the Thugs would chant themselves into a frenzy and then slip into a sort of self-hypnosis. Their priests would carry an odd-looking pickax with a silver blade. They'd communicate using sign language and code phrases. Perhaps some of their people got careless in public. If you don't turn up anything suspicious with Bhowani temples, run a check on temples dedicated to Shiva."

"Shiva?" Sangh glared at the Israeli. "Shiva is one of the great Hindu triad. There are literally *thousands* of temples erected in his honor."

"I know it's quite a task." Katz nodded. "That's what computers are for, to save time on paperwork and filing. Shiva is the god of destruction and recreation. The Thugs believe Kali to be Shiva's daughter. Her powers are supposed to be quite similar to his. It's possible they'd use the father's temple to worship their goddess."

"Anything else?' Sangh asked, almost afraid to voice the question.

"Yeah," the Phoenix Force commander replied. "I want you to contact Mr. Lampert and pass the same request to the NSA. Their SIGINT department likes to keep records on everybody and everything. Let's see if the NSA has any interesting oddities that your section might not have on file."

"Or better yet," McCarter added, "if both CID and NSA have reports of strange activity at the *same* temple."

"Where will you two be?" Sangh inquired.

"We've got a few other things to check on our own," Katz said as he rose from his chair and moved toward the door. "Don't worry. We'll get in touch with you, Colonel."

"I'm sure," Sangh said, his voice filled with resignation.

8

Katz and McCarter met the other members of Phoenix
Force when they returned by helicopter from Calcutta.
They told their teammates the details concerning the incident at the Peacock's Plume. The men of Phoenix
Force were seasoned veterans of numerous covert missions. They had experienced other assignments that
seemed to go sour as soon as they began, but that did not
make them feel any better about the way things seemed
to be going so far in India.

"Shit," Calvin James muttered, expressing everybody's sentiment. "Who would have thought the Thugs
would have agents inside the Indian CID?"

"I should have considered that possibility before Sergeant Din led David and me into a trap," the Israeli
commando replied. "After what we experienced with
the Assassins in the Middle East, I should have suspected something like this might happen."

"Hell, Yakov," Gary Manning sighed. "You're not
Nostradamus. We don't expect you to be able to see into
the future. We don't even expect you to be perfect all the
time."

"Bloody right," McCarter added. "You're almost
always right, Yakov. To tell you the truth, it gets a bit
annoying at times."

Katz smiled, warming to the gruff comradery of his teammates. Phoenix Force was his family, and he loved those four battle-hardened, big-hearted warriors. He would gladly lay down his life for any one of them. Thus far, Phoenix Force had suffered only one casualty. Keio Ohara had been one of the original five members of the team. The tall good-natured Japanese electronics expert had participated in twelve missions before fate claimed his life.

Keio had been the youngest member of Phoenix Force until they recruited Calvin James to the unit. Katz had regarded Ohara as an adopted son. God, how his heart ached even now when he thought of Keio Ohara. Yakov's only son had been killed many years ago in the Middle East. No man should have to bury two sons in one lifetime.

Katz realized he might indeed bury a third. Phoenix Force put their lives on the line every time they set out on mission. Any one or all of them could be killed before they completed their assignment in India. But they were fighting men and this was what they were born to do, as surely as an artist is meant to paint and a writer is meant to write. And none of them would have wanted it any other way.

The five men conversed inside a deserted helicopter hangar at a military airstrip on the outskirts of New Delhi. McCarter glanced about, hoping to find a Coke machine. The Briton had gotten hooked on Coca-Cola during his tours of duty in Southeast Asia and Oman, where a cold drink was more desirable than a beautiful woman. Failing to find what he wanted, McCarter settled for his other favorite vice and fired up a Players.

"Maybe we shouldn't deal with the CID at all," Rafael Encizo suggested. "If the Thugs managed to get one agent inside Sangh's outfit, they've probably got other moles in the organization."

"Well, Lieutenant Tagore and Sgt. Sar Ray didn't lead us into a trap in Calcutta," Manning remarked.

"They haven't *yet*," James replied. "I don't care much for that candy-ass Lampert, but I think I'd feel a little more secure if we were just working with the NSA on this job."

"There might be double agents inside the NSA, as well," Katz stated. "Any organization that gathers covert information in a foreign land has to use native 'cut-outs.' That means there are a lot of Indians on the NSA payroll. Besides, the Thugs aren't the only folks who know how to put a mole in place."

"I think I know what you mean," Encizo commented thoughtfully. "It's funny that all the victims of the Thuggees have been nasty capitalists from the decadent West. I don't care if these guys worship Kali and use silk garrotes instead of pipe bombs and guns. The Thuggees are still acting like terrorists being manipulated by an expert puppet master."

"If that's true," Manning mused, "I'd say the people pulling the strings are either the Chinese SAD or our old sparring partners, the Russian KGB."

"I doubt that the Chinese are responsible," Katz said. "Peking's Social Affairs Department is probably the most underrated intel network in the world; the Chinese are very good at espionage, and they've been doing it successfully for centuries. Still, the Chinese have been trying too hard to make friends with the West lately. If they tried to make a major push into India, they'd screw up some very attractive prospects with the United States and ruin any chance of doing business with Western Europe and Japan."

"The Chinese wouldn't try any bold militaristic action just yet," McCarter declared. "They're a very patient and practical people. Right now, China needs trade and cooperation with more technically advanced countries."

"Okay," Manning said. "Let's assume for a moment the KGB is behind this Thuggee business. Why?"

"India is located between Pakistan and China," Katz began. "India also has lots of internal problems between Hindus and Moslems and militant Sikhs who want a separate country. This country is not in very good political or economic condition. If the KGB can muscle out the West, India will be in even worse shape. Pakistan is run by a military dictatorship that hates India's guts. If India gets weak enough, Pakistan will make its move even if the Russians don't encourage it."

"And if India and Pakistan kick the shit out of each other," Encizo commented, "then the Russians would be able to claim both countries—regardless of who won the war."

"It'd be a sly move, too," McCarter added. "Everybody has been concerned about Soviet activity in Central America and Africa or the Middle East. Nobody's thought too much about the Reds moving into India."

"I'm sure some folks in Moscow have considered it," Katz stated. "If the Soviets could claim both India and Pakistan, they'd have control of the Bay of Bengal, the Indian Ocean and most of the Arabian Sea. Since Soviet puppet governments already control most of Southeast Asia and North Korea, they'd have China covered on all sides."

"That could lead to a very dangerous situation," James remarked. "The type that might involve launching some nuclear missles."

"We might be blowing this whole thing out of proportion," Manning said. "But we'd better take care of these Thuggees PDQ—just in case we've guessed right."

"Great," James groaned. "We might have found the seeds for World War III in India, and we can't trust the people we're forced to work with."

"We can't operate entirely on our own here," Katz responded. "We're pretty much deaf, dumb and blind here without help from insiders. We don't have any choice. We have to work with the NSA and the Indian CID. We just can't trust them too much."

"What about questioning the prisoners being held at CID headquarters?" Encizo suggested. "Abdul and the other Thug?"

"Abdul is in a state of severe shock," Katz replied. "I'm afraid David and I bashed him a bit too hard. The other fellow wasn't hurt much. He's a Hindu and I doubt that he speaks English."

"I'll get Tagore to translate for me," James announced. "Of course, I'll have to check the dude out to see if he's healthy enough to survive a dose of scopolomine. You know, that stuff is the only reliable truth serum, but it can kill a person with a weak heart or respiratory problems."

"Well," the Phoenix Force commander began, "let's get something to eat before we go back to the trenches."

"Hey, I wonder if it's okay to drink the water here," Encizo said.

"We'll let you drink and watch what happens to you, mate," McCarter said with a grin.

"Nice to have friends you can count on," the Cuban said.

CALVIN JAMES EXAMINED THE THUGGEE locked in a cell in the basement jail of the Indian CID building. The medic commando decided the man was too undernourished to survive a potent dose of scopolomine. He also detected a heart murmur. Without proper equipment, James could not be certain how serious this condition might be, and getting proper medical equipment in India is not an easy task.

"Lieutenant Tagore tells me that dude just sits on the floor of his cell and meditates," James told the other members of Phoenix Force as he joined them in a small officers' lounge. "He chants softly, repeating 'Kali' over and over. He won't answer any questions, doesn't respond to threats or even tell the CID if he's hungry or thirsty. I think he's been slapped around a little, too, but either that didn't work or the CID isn't telling us what he said."

"Guy's a fanatic," Encizo commented with a shrug. "You can't break a true zealot that way. We learned that when we tangled with the Assassins."

"He's nuts all right," James confirmed. "Even claims to have seen the goddess Kali, or maybe it was a statue of Kali the goddess had brought to life. Tagore tells me the dude wasn't sure which it was. Said ol' Kali's arms were moving like an octopus in heat."

"Sounds like he'd better stop smoking those funny cigarettes," the Cuban remarked.

"We might have another decent lead, thanks to the computer check by the CID and the NSA," Katz put in.

"Which they wouldn't have done if you hadn't twisted their arms," McCarter growled, but he was in a better mood because he finally had a cold bottle of Coke and Phoenix Force might go into action soon.

"The CID had a police report from Bombay filed away on a floppy disk," Katz told James. "A begger apparently heard voices chanting inside a Bhowani temple. Although it was late at night, the begger decided to enter and ask for alms. Inside, according to this fellow, the temple was full of worshippers. When he called out for alms and extended a palm, somebody grabbed him from behind and began to throttle him with a cord."

"Sounds like somebody doesn't like to be disturbed," Manning commented as he poured himself a cup of coffee.

"The begger said a number of other Bhowani followers approached," Katz continued. "Some of these carried yellow cloth knotted at the center. However, a voice suddenly shouted to assailants to release the begger. Naturally he bolted from the temple and went to the police. Nobody took his story very seriously."

"He was poor and from the wrong caste," James said grimly. "I'm surprised the CID bothered to keep the report."

"I think they still had it on file by accident," Katz replied. "Probably forgot to erase it...fortunately for us."

"Didn't the NSA also have something on the same temple?" Manning asked.

"Yes," the Israeli confirmed. "But it isn't as dramatic. Just a few entries in a computer log about a large number of Bhowani followers congregated in the place between the hours of 10:00 P.M. and four in the morning. NSA thought it might be a covert political rally of some sort, but they weren't terribly interested, either."

"Well," Encizo said with a grin, "sounds like maybe somebody should look into it."

"We will," Katz answered. "But keep in mind that these people might be perfectly innocent. No stormtrooper tactics. We'll find out if these fellows are Thuggees and handle the situation accordingly.''

"We understand," McCarter assured him. "Let's get our gear and pay these blokes a visit."

9

Bombay is one of the largest, most densely populated cities in India. It is also a major seaport and trade center, with the harbors always crowded with ships and boats transporting everything from passengers and luggage to steel and petroleum.

Phoenix Force arrived in Bombay a few hours after sundown, and Lieutenant Tagore accompanied them as the team approached the Temple of Bhowani. The CID officer was only vaguely familiar with Bombay, but he was still better at finding his way around the city than Phoenix Force would have been if they tried to negotiate the crowded streets on their own.

Tagore was a tall gaunt man with a trim black beard and coal-black eyes. He had formerly been a member of the 10th Indian Parachute Battalion and trained as a commando paratrooper. Tagore saw action during the 1971 Bangladesh conflict. He had a good record with the CID, and Phoenix Force had decided Tagore was an unlikely candidate to join the cult of Kali. One reason was that the lieutenant was an atheist.

"The only function of religion is social control," Tagore remarked. "It is supposed to set down spiritual guides for moral and ethical behavior, but in India we have too many different religions, none of which get along. Religion is the cause of half the disputes throughout the world, not just here in India. Look at the Middle East. There is constant fighting between Jews, Moslems and Christians. Or look at Sri Lanka, right at the tip of India. More than half the population are Buddhists and most of the others are Hindus. They're constantly fighting down there. Then the damn Communists get involved in everybody's business. Marxism is virtually a religion without a god, but their zealots are just as fanatic as any other kind of religious lunatic. If there is a God, He must surely be disgusted with the whole lot by now."

Tagore's attitude had not made him popular with his men, who were mostly pious Hindus, but he certainly did not sound like a man who would be in league with the Thuggees. The lieutenant drove a rented Volkswagen minibus past the Temple of Bhowani, and Phoenix Force got their first look at the place.

The temple was made of gray brick with a tar-patch roof and wooden shutters on the windows. Two grim-faced Indians stood guard at the front of the temple. They were dressed in white with yellow turbans on their heads. Neither man appeared to be armed, although they were large enough to physically intimidate anyone who might approach the temple.

"Lieutenant," Katz said, "find a parking space. Somewhere out of view from the temple guards, but not more than a block from the building will be ideal."

"I think we'll find what you want right around the corner," Tagore replied, turning the steering wheel to the right.

The five men of Phoenix Force were dressed in black night-combat uniforms and well armed in case the soft probe turned hard. Katz carried an Uzi submachine gun as well as the SIG-Sauer in shoulder leather. McCarter had his M-10 Ingram and pet Browning holstered under his left arm. Manning had selected a 12-gauge Remington shotgun with an abbreviated barrel and a SWAT-style folding stock. The Canadian also carried a small pack of plastic explosives at the small of his back and a .357 Magnum revolver. James carried a Smith & Wesson Model 76 submachine gun, a favorite weapon of the Navy SEALs, and a .45-caliber Colt Commander.

In addition to a Heckler & Koch MP-5 machine pistol and an S&W Model 59 autoloader, Rafael Encizo carried two knives and three *shaken* throwing stars. The Cuban warrior had a Gerber Mk I fighting dagger clipped to the top of a boot and a Cold Steel Tanto combat knife in a belt sheath. The *shaken* were held in a pouch on Encizo's belt. All five men carried two tear-gas grenades and an M-17 gas mask in a canvas case. Lieutenant Tagore was armed with a Sterling Mk IV subgun and a 9mm FN Browning pistol.

"Mr. Saunders and Mr. Smythe will take out the sentries," Katz said. "Remember, this might be a harmless collection of Hindus worshipping Bhowani. Handle the sentries as innocent bystanders. Don't use deadly force unless there's absolutely no choice. Understand?"

The others nodded.

"Everybody knows what to do," the Phoenix Force commander remarked. "So let's get to work!"

Gary Manning gathered up an Anschütz air rifle and loaded a tranquilizer dart into the breech of the powerful .22-caliber gun. David McCarter, the British pistol champ, armed himself with a Bio-Inoculator. Generally used to capture big game animals alive, the B-I pistol also fired a tranquilizer dart with exceptional accuracy. Both men climbed from the VW minibus and headed for the temple.

McCarter went first because he would have to get closer to his target to use the B-I pistol. The two men were grateful that most of the buildings on the street were jammed together. This created a long, consistent patch of shadows. Manning and McCarter moved along the walls, making the most of the natural camouflage.

One of the guards at the Temple of Bhowani stared at the shadows. McCarter and Manning froze. Their black nightsuits allowed them to blend into the darkness like two chameleons against a tree trunk. The second guard said something to his partner.

Manning raised the Anschütz to his shoulder and gazed through the infrared lens of a telescopic sight mounted on the air rifle. The crosshairs found the side of a sentry's neck, and Manning squeezed the trigger. The Anschütz hissed as it fired a sleep dart. The needle point of the projectile struck on target, and two hundred milligrams of thorazine were injected into the guard's jugular. He pawed at the steel dart lodged in his neck as he stumbled backward and fell against a wall. The guard slumped unconscious to the ground as David McCarter dashed forward.

The Briton dropped to one knee, the B-I pistol held in a two-hand Weaver's combat grip. McCarter snap-aimed and fired. A tranquilizer pierced the second guard's chest. Thorazine pumped into the man's blood, but the sentry remained on his feet. The guy swayed slightly and groaned as he pulled the dart from his chest.

"Bloody hell," McCarter muttered as he charged forward.

The British ace ran toward the disoriented sentry. Gary Manning followed his partner's example. As the guard opened his mouth to shout a warning to the others inside the temple, McCarter suddenly dived forward and hit the ground in a fast shoulder roll. His tumbling body clipped the guard's shins and knocked his feet out from under him.

The guard's cry of alarm became a muffled grunt as he toppled forward. He tried to rise, but Manning closed in swiftly and hammered the bottom of his fist between the man's shoulder blades. The sentry fell flat on his belly. The thorazine took effect, and the man sighed as he slipped into a drugged slumber.

The other members of Phoenix Force and Lieutenant Tagore advanced. Manning and McCarter quickly bound the sentries' ankles and wrists with plastic riot cuffs and dragged them into an alley next to the temple. Calvin James joined the pair while Katz, Encizo and Tagore moved to the opposite side of the building.

Phoenix Force hoped to get enough information about the congregation inside the temple to learn whether or not they were Thuggees. The commando team did not want to burst inside the temple and disturb an innocent group of Hindus carrying out sincere religious services to the goddess Bhowani. They would try to find out as much as possible without using drastic measures.

Katz used a knife blade to pry a slat loose in one of the shutters, raising the wooden vent wide enough to peer inside. Encizo inserted a spike microphone into a crack by the hinge of another shuttered window. The device worked on the same principles of acoustics as placing a drinking glass against a wall. Sound carries through solid objects, and the spike mike received vibrations and amplified the sound through a cord attached to an earplug. Encizo handed the plug to Lieutenant Tagore because he was the only member of the team who understood Hindi.

"They're chanting," the CID man announced in a soft whisper. "Asking the great mother goddess for strength and wisdom, courage and purity. Usual nonsense."

"I see the congregation," Katz whispered as he peered through the space in the window shutter. "Rather a mixed crowd. All different castes appear to be represented."

The Israeli noticed several worshippers wore turbans and cowls. A few were women, but the majority appeared to be Hindu men from the lower castes. The congregation was assembled in a great hall that seemed to take up more than half the building. The interior was dimly lit by candles and the scent of sandalwood incense floated through the slats to Katz's nostrils.

He shifted his head to get a better look at the rest of the worship hall. Katz saw an altar at the end of the room. A priest dressed in a yellow robe and holding a pickax with a silver head addressed the congregation. Beside him on a pedestal was the brass figure of Bhowani—or Kali—with numerous weapons clutched in her eight fists.

"The priest just said, 'Kali demands action, Kali demands sacrifice,'" Tagore told Katz and Encizo. "Now he's talking about how Kali slayed the devils."

"He's referring to the goddess as Kali instead of Bhowani?" Encizo asked eagerly.

"Both names are used for the same goddess," Katz explained. "That doesn't mean they're Thugs, but this is looking more and more suspicious by the second."

"The priest has announced it's time to sacrifice a demon to Kali," Tagore declared.

Katz peered through the peephole as two Indians dragged a white man to the altar. The prisoner's mouth was covered with a gag and each Indian held on to an arm. A third Indian stepped behind the captive and raised a yellow cloth, twisted into a cord and knotted in the middle. Katz quickly took a transceiver from his belt and pressed the button.

"Move in," Katz said urgently. "Now!"

"Affirmative," Gary Manning's voice replied from the radio unit.

Rafael Encizo leaped up to grab the eave of the roof. He swung his body like a pendulum and launched himself feet first at the shuttered window. The flimsy wooden slats burst on impact as the Cuban's feet smashed into the shutters. He plunged through the window and nimbly landed inside the temple among a dozen followers of Kali.

Two startled Indians turned to face the commando who had nearly landed on top of them. Encizo thrust out a boot, kicking a Thuggee as one might a door. The Indian hurtled backward into several other zealots. Another Thug reached for the Cuban as Encizo raised his H&K machine pistol. The Phoenix fighter's left hand chopped his opponent's nearest forearm and swiftly snapped a backfist to the Thuggee's face. She fell to her knees, blood trickling from the nostrils of a broken nose.

Calvin James smashed through another shuttered window at the opposite side of the room. The black warrior literally landed on a Thuggee, his feet slamming into the man's back. The stomp drove the Indian to the floor. James was thrown off balance as more startled Thugs leaped to their feet. The badass from Chicago canted his body in midair to throw a flying body block into two Indians. All three men fell to the floor, with James on top.

The Phoenix pro was on his feet first as two more Indians closed in fast. James slashed the M-76 in a fast backhand sweep, swatting the barrel across an opponent's face. The black tornado whirled with the motion and delivered a tae kwon-do spinning side kick to the other attacker's chest. Both Thuggees fell to the floor as James aimed his Smith & Wesson subgun at the ceiling.

Both Encizo and James fired a volley of 9mm rounds into the ceiling, blasting a shower of plaster dust across the congregation. The Thuggees recoiled from the two machine gunners, backing up toward the center of the prayer hall. Lieutenant Tagore appeared at the window and shouted in Hindi, ordering the Thugs to surrender.

Gary Manning had moved to the front of the temple and placed a six-ounce charge of CV-38 at the door. The Canadian demolitions expert inserted a pencil detonator into the gray puttylike plastic explosive and set the timer for ten seconds. Manning darted to cover. The low-velocity British RDX compound blasted the door open, shattering the bolt. The Canadian combat pro unslung his Remington shotgun from his shoulder and thumbed off the safety as he rushed to the entrance.

The Thuggees stood like a convention of department-store dummies, frozen by surprise rather than fear. The priest yelled at his followers, gesturing with the ornate pickax. None of the members of Phoenix Force understood what he said, but they did not need Tagore to translate.

The two Thuggees who held the white captive did not release him, and the man with the scarf suddenly swung his silk garrote around the prisoner's neck. The strangler crossed his wrists, tightening the scarf and forcing the knot into his victim's windpipe.

Most of the other Thugs attacked the men of Phoenix Force. Only a handful of zealots armed themselves with cloth garrotes. The rest simply lunged forward with fingers arched like claws. They literally attacked the gun-wielding commandos with their bare hands.

"Oh, Jesus!" Calvin James exclaimed when half a dozen fanatics charged toward him.

He hesitated, unwilling to open fire on unarmed opponents. James was a former Golden Gloves boxer and a third *dan* black belt in tae kwon-do, but six against one was still lousy odds, especially when he was pitted against kill-crazy lunatics. He had no choice. James triggered his submachine gun, firing a 3-round burst through the chest of his closest attacker.

James swung his M-76 toward the next opponent, but he had hesitated too long. The Thuggee managed to grab the barrel with both hands and tried to pull the gun from James's grasp. The black warrior squeezed the trigger and shot the Indian in the stomach. The Thug screamed, but held on to the barrel of James's weapon.

Hands clawed at James's arms, pulling hard, and his fingers slipped from the frame of the Smith & Wesson chopper. The gun fell to the floor. A Thuggee gripped each arm and twisted as a third Indian smiled up at the black man. He held a yellow scarf.

James smiled back at the Thug and abruptly spat in his face. The Indian shut his eyes and grimaced as the saliva splattered his features. James quickly launched a snap kick to the Thug's groin. His steel-toed boot crashed into the guy's sex machine with agonizing force. The Thuggee wheezed like a sick cow and clasped both hands to his mashed balls as he wilted to the floor.

Suddenly a streak of yellow flashed past James's eyes. He felt a silk garrote close around his throat. Another

Thuggee had gotten behind him and applied his deadly strangler skills. The other two fanatics still held James's arms as the killer tightened the cord around James's neck. A terrible pressure dug into the black man's windpipe as the knot containing a silver rupee threatened to crush his Adam's apple....

10

David McCarter had drawn his Browning Hi-Power and aimed the pistol with both hands. The British marksman extended his arms through the shattered window and gazed across the special combat sights of his pet handgun. His target was the Thuggee strangler who was throttling the hapless captive who had been chosen for sacrifice by the cult of Kali. McCarter concentrated on this single adversary and failed to notice Calvin James was in the same deadly predicament.

The front sight of the Browning bisected the strangler's head, and McCarter squeezed off a shot. A 115-grain messenger plowed into the side of the Thuggee's skull. The bullet smashed a gory exit hole at the opposite side of the Indian's head, spewing blood and brain matter into the face of another Kali fanatic.

As the man with the perforated skull began to fall, the Thuggee with the faceful of gore released the intended sacrifice to wipe the grisly slime from his eyes. The poor chap who had been throttled slumped to the floor, possibly dead already.

McCarter climbed through the window, holding the Browning in his right fist. Thugs charged at the Briton, two using their empty hands and one holding a silk garrote. McCarter did not hesitate. He promptly shot the closest aggressor, drilling a 9mm hole through the hollow of the bastard's throat.

A yellow cord whipped out and curled around McCarter's wrist like a snake. The Thuggee caught the loose end in his fist and yanked hard. The knotted rupee squeezed, and McCarter cursed under his breath as his fist popped open to drop the Browning autoloader.

"Sneaky bugger," the Briton growled, slashing the side of his left hand into the nerve cluster behind his opponent's collarbone.

The karate blow doubled the man up, and McCarter rammed a knee into the Thug's gut. His moan of pain was music to the Briton's ears as he yanked his right arm to pull the clinging scarf from the Indian's weakened grasp. McCarter slammed his fist into the bloke's face, sending him into an awkward shuffle across the floor.

The third Thuggee lunged at the Phoenix pro's throat, fingers arched like the talons of a murderous vulture. McCarter thrust his arms between the Indian's hands and batted them against the insides of the man's wrist before he could apply a choke hold.

The Briton executed a double thumb jab, stabbing the tips of his thumbs into the carotid arteries of his opponent's neck. The Indian convulsed as if struck by an electric shock. McCarter quickly clapped open palms against the Thug's ears and followed through with a fast karate chop across the bridge of the nose. The Indian fell senseless, but three more Kali zealots launched themselves at McCarter.

"Piss off!" the Briton hissed as he unslung his Ingram machine pistol from his shoulder.

McCarter suddenly dropped to one knee and fired upward, spraying 9mm rounds into his assailants. Three Thugs hopped and twisted in a grim reaper disco step.

Their bullet-torn bodies dropped to the floor in a twitching tangle of arms and legs.

RAFAEL ENCIZO had also been confronted by a tidal wave of Thuggee attackers. The Cuban's childhood had been even more harsh than James's early life in a Chicago ghetto, and he had more experience in hell than the younger black commando. Encizo did not hesitate because his assailants were unarmed, but he was not a cold-blooded killer, either. The Cuban lowered the aim of his MP-5 machine pistol and opened fire.

Nine-millimeter parabellum slugs crashed into the legs and thighs of three Thugs. The trio shrieked in agony and crumpled to the floor, clutching their shattered limbs. Three more Kali crackpots immediately took their places. One Thug even used the squirming body of one of his wounded comrades for a springboard.

The guy literally dived at Encizo, pouncing like a deranged leopard. The Cuban raised his Heckler & Koch blaster and triggered a 3-round burst. Bullets ripped the Thug open from navel to breastbone, but his body collided into Encizo, knocking the H&K machine pistol from the Phoenix warrior's hands.

"Cristo," Encizo muttered as the other two Thugs closed in fast.

They were on him so quickly that he did not have time to draw the S&W Model 59 from shoulder leather. His right hand slapped his belt as a Thuggee swung a silk loop at his head. Encizo's arm rose swiftly, the Cold Steel Tanto in his fist. The razor-sharp edge of the thick six-inch blade slashed the Thug's wrist, nearly chopping his hand off as it sliced through skin and muscle. The blade cut deep into bone, piercing to the marrow.

The Thuggee screamed as blood jetted from severed arteries. His hand dangled uselessly from the maimed wrist and his scarf flapped like a flag of surrender in his other fist. Encizo executed a swift, graceful diagonal stroke with the Tanto. The cut was worthy of a samurai warrior. Encizo's blade sliced the Thug in the side of the neck, severing both the carotid and the jugular before cutting the trachea. The Indian sank to the floor, a crimson volcano flowing from his neck.

The Cuban was so fast and deadly with the knife, the other Thug barely realized what had happened to his comrade. He reached for Encizo as a stream of blood splashed his sleeve. The Indian glanced at the other Kali disciple and saw the scarlet fountain bubbling from the man's neck. The horrifying sight distracted the amateur assassin for a split second.

This was all the time a pro like Rafael Encizo needed. His left hand slashed a cross-body stroke, the hard edge smashing the Thug just above the upper lip. The blow dazed the Indian and made him stagger two steps backward. Then Encizo lunged with the Tanto. The sharp, slanted tip struck the Thuggee under the sternum, piercing the xiphoid process to stab upward into the chest cavity. The Indian gasped in pain and horror as he felt his life begin to seep away.

GARY MANNING had faced another wave of Thugs at the front door. The poker-faced Canadian calmly accepted the challenge and handled it swiftly and efficiently. Like Encizo, Manning lowered the aim of his weapon and fired at his attackers' legs. The semiautomatic Remington shotgun boomed like an angry beast from the depths of hell.

A burst of double O buck transformed a Thuggee's bare foot into crimson jelly. Another blast dissolved a kneecap and took a Kali killer's leg off. A third volley of destruction pulverized most of the muscles in another Indian's thighs. Two pellets to the scrotum would prevent him from fathering any children to be raised as junior Thugs in the future.

A Thuggee wearing a red tuban decided the infidels were not sent as sacrifices for Kali. He clearly intended to shed blood as he hurled himself at Manning, a large curved knife in his fist.

The Canadian raised his Remington and opened fire. Buckshot punched into the knife artist's chest, and the impact hurled the Thuggee six feet to collide with two of his comrades, knocking them to the floor. Another maniac cult member immediately attacked Manning. The Canadian powerhouse glimpsed his assailant and slashed a rapid sweep with the shotgun, slamming the barrel across the idiot's face. The Thug dropped to the floor with a lot of broken bones in his lower face.

A Thuggee suddenly sprang upright, a silk garrote held in his fists. He raised the strangling cloth overhead and tried to rush Manning. The Canadian quickly raised his Remington, holding the shotgun to form a solid bar. The killer's wrists struck the steel frame of Manning's blaster, the yellow scarf flopping harmlessly against the forestock of the Remington. Manning's boot lashed out and caught the guy just above the scrotum. The kick ruptured the Thug's bladder and put a dent in his colon. The Thug folded up in agony, and Manning clubbed him across the back of the skull with the shotgun barrel.

Four hands reached for Manning. The Canadian tried to move back to swing his shotgun at the two attackers, but the Thuggees grabbed the Remington. One Indian seized the barrel while the other held on to the folding stock. The fanatics pulled forcibly, trying to wrench the weapon from Manning's grasp, but the Canadian was built like a young bull and clung to the shotgun.

The muscular Phoenix warrior probably would have won the tug-of-war contest, but he realized other opponents might attack while he was struggling with the two aggressors. Manning suddenly released the shotgun. The two Indians stumbled backward, and the Canadian's hands snaked out. His powerful fingers seized the throats of his enemies and squeezed hard. The Thugs gasped and choked, startled by Manning's unexpected tactic. The Canadian abruptly rolled his brawny shoulders and slammed the Indians' heads together. Their eyes rolled upward, and their bodies fell limp. Manning smacked their skulls together again to be certain both men were unconscious before he released the pair.

CALVIN JAMES had to act quickly. The Thuggee who had wound the silk garrote around his neck was well trained in the art of strangulation. Within seconds, the pressure at his throat would render James senseless or dead. The other two Thugs still held the black man's arms. Nobody was going to save Calvin James except Calvin James.

The black warrior suddenly swung his right leg in a modified roundhouse kick. His muscles extremely flexible from years of tae kwon-do training, James whipped the steel toe of his boot into the face of the Indian who held his left arm. The Thug released James's arm and fell backward, blood oozing from his crushed mouth.

James swung his foot low and stamped it against the shin of the Thug who still held his right arm. The Indian groaned, but did not let go. James grabbed his left fist into the fellow's chin. The blow weakened the Thug's grasp and allowed the Phoenix pro to yank his arm free. James snapped a backfist to the man's face, rapping the big center knuckle right between the Thug's eyes.

The Kali lunatic who still had the scarf around James's neck cursed in Hindi and pulled harder. The black fighting machine reached back over his shoulders and clawed at the strangling cloth, trying to find the Thug's hands. The Indian killer tried to stamp a foot into the back of James's knee. The kick scraped the black man's calf muscle. James responded by stomping a heel into the Thug's instep. The strangler grunted and twisted the garrote, trying to pull James off balance.

Then the Phoenix commando found the Thuggee's hands. He pried at the man's fists until he caught both little fingers. In the movies, a hero might throw the strangler over his shoulder. In reality, this would probably result in a broken neck. James concentrated on his opponent's little fingers, bending them back until bones snapped.

The Thug cried out in pain, and James twisted the broken fingers viciously, forcing the killer to release his garrote. The black warrior thrust the back of his heel upward and drove it between the Thug's splayed legs. The Indian rasped in a high-pitched whine. James quickly rammed the point of his elbow to his opponent's jaw and knocked the Thuggee to the floor in a senseless heap.

However, the other two Thugs had only been dazed and they were mad as hell because James refused to be a cooperative sacrifice. One Indian closed in and rammed a fist to the black man's stomach. James grunted, but managed to raise his right forearm to block the clawing fingers that reached for his bruised throat.

The Phoenix crusader jabbed his left fist at the Thug's mouth and followed with a left hook to the side of his jaw. The Indian staggered back from the punches. Cal caught him under the jaw with a right uppercut, and the man's head bounced back, exposing his throat. James swiftly slashed the side of his hand across the Thug's windpipe. The Indian tumbled to the floor, choking to death from a crushed thyroid cartilage.

Fingers clawed into James's hair from behind. The Thug assailant planned to pull James's head back to get an arm around his throat, but the black man pumped an elbow into the attacker's solar plexus and turned sharply. Pain lanced his scalp as the Thug held on to his hair, and James knocked the man's arm aside with a rising block and hammered his right fist under the Indian's ribs. The Kali cultist moaned and shuffled away from James.

The black man did not let his opponent get very far. He launched a kick at the Indian's groin, and the Thug reached for James's leg, hoping to throw him off balance. But the kick was a feint, and James pulled the attack short and abruptly swung his foot in a fast roundhouse kick. The boot crashed into the side of the Indian's skull. The stunned cultist fell to his knees, and James quickly stepped closer and snapped a backfist to his opponent's face. The guy sprawled on his back with a sigh, as if glad to slide into unconscious oblivion.

THE PRIEST IN CHARGE of the Bombay chapter of the Thuggees had ordered his followers to fight the infidels, but he and his two personal bodyguards chose to flee from the temple. The priest's enforcers reached under their robes and drew their old British Enfield revolvers as the trio ran for the rear exit of the building.

One guard lingered in the worship hall to fire a hasty shot at Lieutenant Tagore. The CID officer had climbed through the window, his Sterling Mk IV held ready. The Thuggee's .38 round hissed within inches of Tagore's right shoulder. The bullet struck the windowsill behind the lieutenant, splintering wood and ricocheting against the brick base beneath.

Tagore instantly returned fire. His Sterling subgun spat a rapid-fire volley of 9mm slugs that sliced a diagonal line of bullet holes in the Thuggee's chest. The bodyguard was hurled into the altar of Kali by the impact of the multiple parabellum slugs. His corpse fell against the statue of the goddess, knocking the brass figure to the floor.

The priest and the surviving bodyguard retreated into a narrow passage and headed for the exit. Colonel Yakov Katzenelenbogen had already found the rear door from outside the temple, and the Kali priest and his henchman ran for safety only to find the Phoenix Force commander waiting for them.

The Thuggee bodyguard raised his .38 Enfield, but Katz triggered his Uzi before the gunman could aim his revolver, let alone fire it. Two 9mm rounds slammed into the man's chest and throat while a third smashed through his teeth to hiss inside the fellow's mouth before shattering neck vertebrae.

The priest cried out in horror as he saw his bodyguard fall dead at his feet. A portly, middle-aged Indian, the priest stared fearfully at Katz. He clutched the ritual pickax as if hoping its magic would ward off the formidable figure who stood before him. But the man with the compact machine gun and a hand made of steel hooks remained.

"It is said every smart businessman in India must learn at least three languages," Katz declared. "Do you speak English?"

"Yes, sahib," the priest replied with a humble bow. "Please do not kill me. I am not a man of violence, and I would rather reward you with silver than continue this carnage."

"I am not interested in silver," the Israeli said.

"But you shall have it, anyway," the priest told him.

With surprising speed for a man of his bulk, the priest slashed the pickax in a cross-body stroke. The silver blade flashed toward Katz's head, but the Israeli was faster. He raised his prosthesis, and the steel limb blocked the bamboo shaft of the ornate pickax.

Katz swiftly slammed the frame of his Uzi down on the priest's right hand, smashing the man's fingers. The Thug leader screamed, but Katz ignored him and clamped the hooks of his prosthesis around the fellow's left wrist. He flexed the muscles of his stump to manipulate the device, tightening the steel talons with bone-crushing force.

The priest shrieked as his wrist was pulverized in the vicelike grip. The pickax fell to the floor, and Katz kicked one of the Thug's feet, tripping the man. The priest crashed on his back, sobbing with pain.

"Look," Katz said as he gazed down at the cultist, "we don't have all night. Get up so we can wrap our business here."

11

"Your tactics are most distressing, Mr. Jacobs," Colonel Sangh said with a sigh. "A gun battle in the middle of Bombay! You can't just run about killing people this way!"

"Then how should we be killing people?" David McCarter asked with a sneer as he lighted a Players cigarette.

"Take it easy, Smythe," Katz said, using McCarter's cover name. "You'll give poor Colonel Sangh a heart attack."

Katz, McCarter and Encizo were meeting with Sangh in the CID man's office. Manning, James and Lieutenant Tagore were interrogating several captives from the Temple of Bhowani. Although the majority of the Thuggees had survived the gun battle, many of them were badly injured. They were either suffering from shock or pumped full of drugs. So Phoenix Force concentrated on questioning the Thugs who were still in relatively good physical condition.

"The Bombay police are very upset about this incident," Sangh declared. "One doesn't raid a house of worship in India. Religion is very important here. Many of our people live only for their religion. The structure of our society is founded on faith. Launching an attack on a temple is most unseemly."

"It was unseemly when the Thugs started to strangle a guy as a sacrifice to Kali," Encizo said with a yawn. "Freedom of religion in India doesn't include ritual murder...I hope."

"Of course not," Sangh replied. "But law enforcement in India must be concerned with public relations. Religious disputes have caused violence in India before. Militant Sikhs want their own country, separate from the rest of India. This resulted in many acts of terrorism in recent years. There were accusations that the government under Mrs. Gandhi persecuted the Sikhs."

"From what I understood, those accusations weren't totally unfounded," McCarter said dryly.

"Perhaps," Sangh admitted. "But the situation in India certainly became worse when fanatic Sikhs murdered Mrs. Gandhi. At the moment the tension between Hindu and Sikh has tapered off. Yet tales of more government action against religious sects could bring them to the boiling point again."

"We appreciate your situation, Colonel Sangh," Katz assured him. "But the Thuggee conspiracy might prove to be a far greater threat to India than you realize. In fact, it may be the beginning of a plot that could endanger the safety of the entire world."

"How melodramatic," Sangh commented. "And what proof have you of this theory, Mr. Jacobs?"

"Not enough to convince you, Colonel," the Phoenix Force commander confessed. "At least not yet."

"Look, Colonel," Encizo began, waving some of McCarter's smoke away from his face with annoyance. "We didn't want to shoot it out with the Thugs. We intended to make it a recon mission, but when we discovered they were about to sacrifice an innocent man to Kali, we had to stop them. Even then we tried to take them without bloodshed, but they attacked us. There were more than thirty Thuggees in the temple, so we had to use our weapons."

"This fellow the Thuggees were about to strangle," Sangh began. "You took him to the American Embassy, correct?"

"He had been choked unconscious before Mr. Smythe killed the man who was strangling him," Katz explained. "We revived him and discovered his name is Charles Bricker. Dr. Bricker to be exact. He's attached to the U.S. Embassy, but he came to India to help treat victims of the Union Carbide disaster who suffered long-term respiratory damage to lungs and such. He's been living in New Delhi, although he's been making house calls to the homes and clinics where these unfortunates are staying."

"We'll need a statement from Dr. Bricker," Sangh declared.

"I contacted Waldo Lampert," Katz continued. "He'll meet with Bricker. He'll get a statement from the doctor, and he'll check Bricker's personnel file to make certain he isn't CIA or NSA in disguise."

"Does that make a difference?" Sangh inquired.

"It might," the Israeli replied. "We have to cover every possibility, Colonel."

Gary Manning and Lieutenant Tagore wearily entered the office. Encizo poured some black coffee into a cup and handed it to the Canadian. Manning thanked him and gratefully gulped down some hot brew.

"Looks like you've had a hard day's night," Encizo said with a grin. "Wear yourself out swinging a rubber hose?"

"Funny," Manning said sourly. "You ought to go down there and help interrogate a bunch of psychos.

Even with the scopolomine, those guys don't make any sense."

"Sometimes the truth doesn't seem to make sense," Katz remarked. "What did you learn from our prisoners, Mr. Saunders?"

Manning slumped into a chair. "The Thugs chanted a lot," Manning said. "They ignored our questions and kept chanting and praying until Cal...er, Mr. Jones injected truth serum into them. We questioned seven Thugs under the influence of scopolomine. Might as well have talked to just one."

"They must have said something important," Sangh commented, frowning.

"We asked them where the headquarters of the cult of Kali is located," Manning replied. "Every one of the Thugs told us it was at something called mountain of Kali. Okay, so where is the mountain of Kali? The answer: every Thug claimed they were blindfolded and handcuffed before being taken to the site of the 'mother goddess.' They arrived at the foot of the mountain where the 'Man without a name' leads the services."

"The man without a name?" Encizo raised his eyebrows. "Sounds like a character from an Italian Western."

"The translation is actually 'the Nameless One,'" Lieutenant Tagore explained. "The Thugs were referring to their supreme high priest. He is nameless because he speaks for the goddess Kali."

"Yeah," Manning said. "But here's the fun part. The Thugs all claim they actually *saw* Kali in the flesh. Well, flesh isn't exactly accurate. They described her as resembling a statue that had been brought to life. They claim they saw Kali's arms move and her head turn from side to side."

"Interesting," Katz mused. "One of the Thugs from the Peacock's Plume told the same story."

"But he didn't claim he saw Kali kill without shedding blood," the Canadian remarked.

"What?" Encizo stared at Manning. "They said they actually saw Kali strangle someone?"

"Why not?" McCarter snorted. "With eight arms she ought to be able to hold a victim and strangle him while she's combing her hair and talking to a chum on the telephone all at the same time."

"The Thugs said Kali destroyed a 'British monster' with a fiery beam of holy light," Tagore explained. "The light supposedly dissolved bones and flesh. Of course it did not shed a drop of blood."

"But this is the most important part," Manning stated. "They said a Russian soldier was standing right beside the Englishman when Kali zapped him with the holy death ray. Apparently the demonstration was to show the Thugs that Kali wants her followers to spare the Russians."

"Isn't that interesting," Encizo mused. "An Indian goddess who approves of Soviet Communists."

"This is beginning to make sense," Katz commented.

"I'm glad you think so," Tagore sighed. "It's all silly rubbish from opium addicts if you ask me."

"But the Soviets are to be spared," McCarter stated. "Now there has to be a reason for that."

"Spared by a goddess who shoots a fiery light that dissolves human beings?" Colonel Sangh remarked, shaking his head. "The whole thing sounds like a legend that the Thugs had convinced themselves is the truth."

"But there is a kind of concentrated light that can burn through solid steel," Katz declared. "Or human flesh for that matter."

"A laser," Manning supplied. "I thought of that, too, but this business about an eight-armed living goddess..."

"That resembled a statue," Katz reminded him. "A statue that moves and sounds like a stop-action animated figure in a movie, correct? Standard special effects. But in this case, the Russians are probably using a mechnical device."

"The goddess Kali is a robot?" Tagore asked with astonishment.

"Something like that," the Israeli replied. "A mechanical figure with a built-in laser cannon."

"But could they fit all those gears and circuits into a robot and still have room for a laser gun?" Manning wondered aloud.

"Witnesses said Kali moved her arms and head," Katz said. "What's complicated about that? Clockwork figures do the same thing. That sort of technology has been around since the eighteenth century. Doing the same thing with an electric motor would be child's play to a modern engineer."

"Wait a moment," Sangh urged. "You gentlemen believe the Russians are responsible for the Thuggees?"

"Let's say the Kremlin and the KGB," Katz replied. "I'm of Russian descent myself. The Russian people didn't want communism. It was thrust upon them after the czar was dethroned. At first, communism appeared to be an improvement, but it turned out to be another form of tyranny. Believe me, most Russians love their country with a passion, and they hate the repressive liars who run their government with terror tactics and secret police."

"A KGB plot with a mechanical goddess?" Sangh shook his head. "It's too incredible. How are you going to convince anyone such a thing has happened?"

"Not *has* happened," Encizo corrected. "It's happening *now*. We've put a small group of Thugs out of business, but that won't be enough to make the KGB close up shop in India. They've kept tight security. None of the Thugs know where the mountain of Kali is located. Their claims of magic and mystical orders from a legendary goddess would be laughed out of any serious investigation. The KGB doesn't have anything to worry about yet."

"The problem is," Katz went on, "when the Soviets realize we're getting close to exposing their scheme, the KGB will disappear faster than a soldier's virginity."

"We're not close enough to worry them yet," Manning remarked. "Frankly I don't see how we're going to get much closer. Sure as hell won't get any more information from the Thuggees."

"Maybe we should try a different angle," the Israeli announced. "Let's get some sleep. Tomorrow we'll see if Lampert and the NSA can supply us with some new information."

"About the Thuggees?" Sangh inquired.

"No," Katz replied. "The KGB."

THE FOLLOWING MORNING Yakov Katzenelenbogen, Gary Manning and Rafael Encizo joined Waldo Lampert in a conference room inside the American Embassy in New Delhi. The lights were off as the National Security Agency case officer ran a slide projector, consulting his notes as magnified pictures appeared on the screen.

"Okay," Lampert began. "As I'm sure you guys know, the Soviets generally slip their KGB agents into other countries through their embassies. Of course, every intel outfit uses this technique to some degree. Now the NSA and CIA try to keep tabs on Russian personnel at the embassies. We keep a special eye peeled for known or suspected KGB agents.''

''I'm sure the Russians watch our embassy just as carefully,'' Encizo, a naturalized U.S. citizen, remarked. ''I'm glad we entered the embassy disguised as maintenance workers.''

''We try to cover everything,'' Lampert replied. ''Here's a face of interest that was photographed outside the Soviet embassy.''

A thin face with sunken cheeks and deep-set dark eyes appeared on the screen. He wore a straw hat, but a fringe of white hair poked from under the headgear. The man's nose was hooked with a small trim mustache on his upper lip.

''Sergei Ivanovich Tikhonov,'' Lampert announced. ''Professor Tikhonov, to be exact. Probably the leading authority on laser research in the Soviet Union. Helped build the first industrial laser for the Russians in the early sixties. Also involved in laser research for surgical purposes. However for the past five years Tikhonov has been working on laser weaponry. Part of the Soviet program for killer satellites and advanced antitank and antiaircraft devices.''

''And he's in India?'' Manning inquired.

''He was,'' Lampert explained. ''This photograph was taken in July. Tikhonov was in India for about six months, spending most of the time in Calcutta. He flew back to the Soviet Union and, according to SIGINT sources, the professor was reported in Bulgaria just last month.''

"Any information about what Tikhonov was doing in Calcutta?" Yakov asked, firing up a Camel.

"Even SIGINT couldn't turn up anything definite," Lampert answered, changing slides. "However, we know a number of other Soviet personnel were in Calcutta and the Bengal region at the time. Including this interesting character."

Another face appeared on the screen. It was the face of a proud man with a lantern jaw and sky-blue eyes. His light brown hair was trimmed short and was gray at the temples. Even in the photograph, the face expressed determination and strong-willed ambition.

"Maj. Mikhail Fedorovich Yousopov," Lampert declared. "KGB case officer, Foreign Intelligence Division, Special Operations Section sometimes known as Septsburo. Quite a file on this guy, not a lot of information, but all of it is impressive. In the early sixties, Yousopov participated in the Olympics. Wrestling. He was pretty good, too. No bronze medal, but damn close. Must have been recruited into the KGB immediately afterward. Showed up in India during the early seventies, probably connected with the Madras Independence Front leftist terrorists. After that, he must have returned to Moscow for a while. He showed up in Afghanistan a couple years ago. Our intel isn't complete in that part of the world these days, but Yousopov appeared to be in charge of a bunch of stool pigeons who informed on Afghan freedom fighters."

"Nice assignment," Enzico commented. "Does Yousopov keep pet maggots for a hobby?"

"The records don't have much on personal details," Lampert replied. "But Yousopov must have made his masters in the KGB happy because they promoted him to major and let him handle even more informers. Major Yousopov then wound up in India."

"With a laser expert," Manning remarked. "Is Yousopov still in India?"

"I hate to admit it," Lampert sighed, "but we're not sure. The KGB sometimes manages to slip agents in and out of the country without our knowledge. We're not certain about a number of the other Russians who were in Calcutta at that time. SIGINT got very little information. Little more than a few photographs."

"Were any of these other Russians KGB?" Katz inquired.

"Most of them were young," Lampert answered. "To be honest, we have very little on record about them. They entered the country through the embassy and listed their occupation as construction workers and engineers in the Soviet army. Others were supposedly electricians, radio commo personnel and computer technicians. However, one of these engineers was indeed someone special."

Lampert worked his projector again. A new face appeared on the screen. A middle-aged man with a wide smile and plump cheeks gazed down at them. His nose was wide and dark with broken blood vessels. He looked like a good-natured Ukrainian peasant who was a bit too fond of vodka.

"Professor Nikolai Nikanorovich Striganov," Lampert said. "One of the top designers and engineers in the Soviet Union. This fellow has done some work for the Russian space program. Helped to design a robot arm for work in outer space. He also worked on a 'lunar rover' vehicle designed to travel on the surface of the moon. Of course the Russians haven't made it to the moon yet, but this contraption by Striganov was pretty clever. Robot arms for taking rock and soil samples, a crane device for lifting heavy objects and even tripod 'feet' to climb over surfaces the tractor wheels can't manage.''

''Sounds like he wouldn't have any trouble at all building a statue of Kali with mechanical arms,'' Manning commented.

''Striganov flew back to the Soviet Union months ago,'' Lampert said. ''But he was in India long enough to complete construction of something like that—assuming your theory is accurate. The other engineers and technicians who can't be accounted for could certainly carry on without Striganov after the thing was constructed.''

''All right,'' Katz said, crushing the life from his cigarette in a glass ashtray. ''NSA doesn't have any details concerning what the Soviets were doing in India, but you seem to know a great deal about the Russians involved. I assume you know where they stayed while in Calcutta.''

''They rented a building,'' Lampert answered as he switched on the lights. ''Calcutta is pretty much the business center of India. Nothing illegal about renting a building. And the Soviets had diplomatic immunity because they were connected with the embassy. The Indians are like people everywhere. They don't like messing with VIPs who have diplomatic immunity.''

''Does your file tell us what company rented the building to the Russians?'' Manning asked.

''Let's see,'' the NSA man began, checking his files. ''Oh, God. It wasn't a company. Rajput Ram Somnoka owns the place. He personally rented the building to the Soviets.''

''Who's the guy?'' Encizo asked. ''Somebody important?''

DYNAMITE OFFER!

4 EXPLOSIVE NOVELS PLUS SUNGLASSES FREE

delivered right to your home with no obligation to buy—ever

TAKE 'EM FREE

4 action-packed novels and a rugged pair of sunglasses

With an offer like this, how can you lose?

Return the attached card, and we'll send you 4 adventure novels just like the one you're reading plus a pair of sunglasses — ABSOLUTELY FREE.

If you like them, we'll send you 6 books every other month to preview. Always before they're available in stores. Always for less than the retail price. Always with the right to cancel and owe nothing.

NON-STOP HIGH-VOLTAGE ACTION

As a Gold Eagle subscriber, you'll get the fast-paced, hard-hitting action you crave. Razor-edge stories stripped to their lean muscular essentials. Written in a no-holds-barred style that keeps you riveted from cover to cover.

In addition you'll receive...

- our free newsletter AUTOMAG with every shipment
- special books to preview free and buy at a deep discount

RUSH YOUR ORDER TO US TODAY

Don't let this bargain get away. Send for your 4 free books and sunglasses now. They're yours to keep even if you never buy another Gold Eagle book.

Mean up your act with these tough sunglasses

Unbeatable! That's the word for these tough street-smart shades. Durable metal frame. Scratch-resistant acrylic lenses. Fold 'em into a zip pouch and tuck 'em in your pocket. Best of all, they're yours free.

FREE BOOKS & SUNGLASSES

YEAH, send my 4 **free** Gold Eagle novels plus my **free** sunglasses. Then send me 6 brand-new Gold Eagle novels (2 **Mack Bolans** and one each of **Phoenix Force, Able Team, Track** and **SOBs**) every second month as they come off the presses. Bill me at the low price of $1.95 each (for a total of $11.70 per shipment—a saving of $2.30 off the retail price). There are no shipping, handling or other hidden charges. I can always return a shipment and cancel at any time. Even if I never buy a book from Gold Eagle, the 4 free books and the sunglasses (a $6.95 value) are mine to keep.

166 CIM PAGV

NAME_____

ADDRESS_____ APT._____

CITY_____

STATE_____ ZIP_____

Offer limited to one per household and not valid for present subscribers. Prices subject to change.

PRINTED IN U.S.A

JOIN FORCES WITH GOLD EAGLE'S HEROES

- Mack Bolan...lone crusader against the Mafia and KGB
- Able Team...3-man combat squad blitzes global terrorism
- Phoenix Force...5 mercenaries battle international crime
- Track...weapons genius stalks madman around the world
- SOBs...avengers of justice from Vietnam to Iran

For free offer, detach and mail

"A rajput is the son of a maharaja," Lampert explained. "The guy is Indian royalty. Prince Ram is heir to the position of the third largest maharaja clan in West Bengal."

"I thought the maharajas fell from grace even before the British pulled out of India," Encizo remarked.

"They don't have any political authority," Lampert answered. "But they still have influence. Royal birth is royal birth, and the government tries to get along with the maharajas and rajputs."

"We'll try to be diplomatic when we talk to Prince Ram," Katz assured him.

"Oh, no," Lampert groaned. "I don't think you should..."

"We'll fly to Calcutta as soon as possible, Mr. Lampert," Katz told him. "Can you arrange an NSA contact in the city if we need one?"

"Yeah," Lampert said, misery in his tone. "I just hope you guys know what you're doing."

"We try," Encizo said cheerfully. "Oh, any messages you'd like us to give the prince?"

Lampert muttered something under his breath, but whatever it was, he did not bother to repeat it.

12

Ranjit Nangal decided Australia would be an ideal place to start his new life. The little Indian had heard conflicting stories about the Land Down Under. Some said Australians did not welcome dark-skinned foreigners. Others said Australians were friendly toward everyone, regardless of color. Nangal did not worry. A rich man is welcome anywhere, regardless of his skin shade or ethnic background.

Money talks a universal language of respect. Nangal had learned this lesson as a child. The rich did their best to keep the wealth limited to themselves in India. They married into one another's families. They gave financial support to the candidates who best represented their interests. They gave lip service to the plight of the poor and generally blamed conditions on the oppressive British, whose regime in India had ended almost forty years ago, or on the selfish capitalist Americans who had only given India a couple of billion dollars in foreign aid when everybody knew they could afford to give trillions.

Nangal had also noticed that the most honored and respected of all the higher castes were the priests and other religious leaders. The most famous and influential leader in India had undoubtedly been Mahatma Gandhi. He was not known for his wealth or his strategic wisdom but for his spiritual insight. He was more a religious leader than a statesman. Even the British had feared him, although Gandhi preached nonviolence. Of course, the British had not wished to slaughter millions of Indians to crush Gandhi's following. Nangal often wondered what would have happened if Gandhi had used such tactics with Adolf Hitler.

The Nazis would have killed Gandhi and anyone who supported him. They would have burned Indian pacifists in ovens or marched them into gas chambers. Nangal suspected Mahatma Gandhi would have become an obscure martyr under those conditions. Indians still quoted Gandhi, and his memory was honored and praised throughout the world. But what had happened to the united India of Gandhi's dream, of his hopes for a self-sufficient and peaceful India?

Hindu, Moslem and Sikh remained bitter enemies. India could not feed its people or clothe its poor. Since Gandhi's death India had gone to war with Pakistan and been plagued with internal violence and terrorism. All that Gandhi had stood for did not last in India. Pacifism might be a lofty principle, but it certainly did not make successful long-term politics.

Yet Gandhi was still beloved and respected because he had been a religious leader who took a political stand. Every religion in India honored Gandhi, although few practiced what he taught. The English even made movies with Gandhi as the hero and the British as villains. In America, other religious leaders copied Gandhi's example and became more involved in political and social movements. One of these Christian leaders ran for president.

The benefits of being a religious leader were many. It was a way for a man to become wealthy, powerful and famous. Nangal had no interest in fame. He would be happy just to be rich and powerful.

However, Nangal had not planned to revive the Cult of the Thuggees. He had originally formed a rather small sect of gullible young idiots who regarded him as a guru teaching spiritual oneness with the universe. Nangal's religious training also consisted of making his followers surrender all worldly possessions. Naturally they gave this earthly trash to the guru to dispose of. They were also forced to go days without eating or sleeping. They learned monotonous chants and complex rituals.

After his followers had become totally brainwashed into following the guru's every order, Nangal sent them out to steal for him. The religious thieves brought their leader numerous wallets, rings, watches and assorted jewelry. The plan seemed to be working out fine until one of his thieves handed Nangal a Russian passport.

In less than an hour the Russians had located Nangal's little cult. Five angry "diplomats" from the Soviet embassy had kicked down the door. The Russians had silencers on their pistols so they could shoot down Nangal's followers without making too much noise. Then one of the Soviet gunmen aimed his weapon at Nangal's sweat-covered face.

"You're the leader, aren't you?" the Russian asked in accented Hindi.

"No, no," Nangal replied, his teeth chattering with terror. "I am innocent..."

"No one is innocent," the gunman said with a smile. "I have no use for an innocent man who would bear witness to our actions. However, a shrewd false prophet who can convince Indians that committing crimes is a religious experience...such a man may indeed be useful to me."

"All right," Nangal sobbed, closing his eyes so he would not see the shot that was about to kill him. Yet he had nothing to lose by confessing. "I am a guru."

"Good," Major Yousopov said as he lowered his gun. "I want to make you an offer, and if you want to live you won't refuse."

This was the beginning of Nangal's partnership with the KGB. The Soviets needed a false guru for their plot to revive the Thuggees. Nangal was perfect for the role. Now, almost two years later, the Cult of Kali numbered more than three hundred. The scarf-wielding killers stalked their prey from one end of India to the other. They blindly carried out the orders of their goddess and the words of their holy leader, Ranjit Nangal.

The Russians were clever, Nangal admitted. They had made Kali move and turn her head. The laser beam was a brilliant addition that certainly made an impression on ignorant Indians who thought nuclear energy was similar to coal and cars were powered by small animals hidden beneath the hood. But the KGB could never have put the cult together without Nangal. Major Yousopov needed him and they both knew it.

However, Nangal's instincts told him it would soon be time to get the hell out. The farther away he could get from West Bengal, the better. Australia ought to be far enough, and with a fortune in gold Nangal could live like a king for the rest of his life without working another scam again.

"Nangal!" Major Yousopov shouted from the control center inside Kali mountain. "Come here, damn you! We've got a problem."

"What's wrong, Comrade Major?" Nangal asked with a smile as he entered the room. "Did the goddess blow a fuse?"

"I'm in no mood for your stupid jokes, Nangal," the KGB officer snapped. "I've just received a radio message from an intelligence source in Bombay. The section of Thuggees stationed there at the Temple of Bhowani has been wiped out. Every single Thug there was either killed or captured during a raid last night."

"That's impossible," Nangal said with astonishment. "I can't imagine the Bombay police carrying out a raid on a Hindu temple, and the CID had been leaving the investigation of the Thuggee killings in the hands of the local police."

"Not anymore," Yousopov snapped. "Not since those five professional troublemakers arrived from the United States. One of our informers inside the CID told us about them, remember? You ought to. That idiot Sergeant Din was one of your flunkies."

"Don't blame that on me, Major," Nangal said defensively. "Din took it upon himself to lure those two Americans into a trap at the Peacock's Plume. He probably thought he was very clever. Frankly you can't blame him for being confident that the trap would work. Seven men against two seems like good enough odds to be sure of the outcome."

"That depends on who the two men are," Yousopov said grimly. "These five men from America are special. If they assaulted the base in Bombay, I'm not surprised the Thugs were wiped out."

"Do you know who these men are?" Nangal asked.

"Do I know their names or even their nationalities?" Yousopov said with a shrug. "No. However, there have been reports coming into the Communications Directorate Division of the KGB about a five-man commando team. They ruined an operation in the United States some time ago. I don't know any details, but it had something to do with crippling the Americans' nuclear power. Five men ruined the scheme. Five highly trained professionals.''

''But that's no reason to believe the same five men are here in India,'' Nangal replied.

''If that was the only incident, I'd agree,'' Yousopov answered. ''However, we had another major operation in Greece. A Bulgarian was in charge of the mission, but it was a KGB operation. Security was very tight, and I heard even less about it than the mission in America. But I know it involved Krio Island and the operation was destroyed by five men. Most recently another KGB mission in Turkey was smashed by a commando raid. Once again five men were involved in the incident. Five professionals, experts in espionage, infiltration and virtually every form of combat short of nuclear warfare.''

''You still can't be sure these are the same men,'' Nangal said, surprised that Yousopov seemed so worried about this possibility.

''The descriptions of the team varies,'' the major stated, talking to himself more than Nangal. ''But more than one report mentioned a middle-aged man with an artificial arm. Some of the early intel information indicated an Oriental was part of the team. A tall man, probably Japanese. But the more recent observations suggest a black man has joined the unit. The director of the KGB is personally concerned about this matter. The premier himself has warned us to beware of this elite commando team.''

''Major Yousopov,'' Nangal said, shaking his head. ''Even if these fellows are the superwarriors you mentioned, they're just men. Not devils or evil spirits. That's the sort of rubbish the superstitious retards in our cult believe in. We have a small army of assassins. Certainly they can take care of five men."

"These commandos are professional fighting men," Yousopov told him. "They're armed with automatic weapons. Your Thuggees will never get close enough to use those silk scarf garrotes."

"What do you suggest?" Nangal asked. "I suppose you could send some of your Russian paratroopers after them."

"I'm certain my men would be more than a match for this American gangster squad if they were to fight in open combat," Yousopov declared. "But my people don't speak Hindi or Urdu. Besides, they aren't espionage agents or trained assassins. They couldn't handle this job discreetly. The Soviet Union doesn't want an international incident in India."

"You're probably worried about nothing, Major," Nangal told him. "If these chaps are in Bombay or New Delhi they aren't even close to our headquarters."

"I'm not taking any chances," Yousopov declared. "I'll alert that bandit chief Bahir Khan to watch out for invaders. No one will associate an attack by Moslem hill bandits with the Cult of Kali."

"I suppose that's true," Nangal agreed.

"Now," Yousopov continued, "the only way they could find out where we are is through that pompous monarch ass, Prince Ram. I want you to send your best men to make certain Ram's property is well protected."

"By my 'best men' you can't mean Chopera and Kosti?" the Thuggee leader demanded. "They're my priests. I need them here."

"You were leading the Cult of Kali before they joined us," Yousopov stated. "You can get along without them now. It is vital that we have competent people in charge of security at Ram's palace.''

"Chopera and Kosti aren't security experts,'' Nangal said. "They're former hoodlums pretending to be holy men."

"They're cold-blooded killers,'' Yousopov declared. "And that's exactly what I want at Ram's place. If our enemies show their faces there, I don't want ritual strangulation or silly ceremonies. I want them dead. Nothing fancy. Just kill them and make certain every one of those bastards is dead."

13

Phoenix Force needed a large enough aircraft to transport the entire team, including Lieutenant Tagore, and all their equipment. They traveled north of New Delhi to the ancient city of Delhi to board a military C-130, and began their journey to Calcutta.

The largest city in the West Bengal region, Calcutta was the setting for the infamous "Black Hole of Calcutta," where almost one hundred fifty British captives were apparently crammed into a cell eighteen feet long and fourteen feet wide, with only one small window. Supposedly only twenty-three prisoners survived the ordeal.

Robert Hislaw met Phoenix Force and Lieutenant Tagore at the airstrip. A Sioux Indian from South Dakota, Hislaw was a tall lean man with copper-brown skin and proud features. Hislaw was the top NSA case officer in West Bengal.

"I guess the National Security Agency figured one kind of Indian would fit in as well as any other," Hislaw told Phoenix Force after they completed initial introductions. No one was quite certain if Hislaw was joking or serious.

"We've been told you're one of the best NSA operatives in the field," Katz replied as they followed Hislaw into a hangar. "And you're the best man to tell us about Rajput Ram Somnoka."

"Not much thrilling info on the guy," Hislaw said with a shrug. "Ram is the son of Maharaja Morarji Somnoka. The eldest son, which makes him heir to the throne, something that doesn't make the maharaja very happy."

"They don't get along?" Rafael Encizo inquired as he laid a duffel bag full of gear on the floor.

"Not at all," Hislaw confirmed. "The maharaja is pretty much a traditional Hindu. Worships the great triad—Brahma the Creator, Vishnu the Preserver and Shiva the Destroyer. Prince Ram has been drifting to and from different cult groups. He even attended Buddhist ceremonies for a while. Funny thing is the prince has a nasty streak a mile wide and two miles long. Ram was accused of sexual assault, assault and battery and conspiracy to commit murder, but nobody could ever get enough evidence to make the charges stick. In India, you don't arrest a rajput without a ton of evidence."

"Maybe Ram has been trying to find a religion that will help him control his evil temper," Manning suggested.

"Or one that will allow him to exercise it," McCarter mused. "The bloke would fit right in with the Cult of Kali."

"Yeah," Hislaw agreed. "The Thuggees. Well, Somnoka, Jr., has his own private estate, and the place is crawling with odd characters. The NSA didn't care much what Ram was up to until he rented that warehouse to the Russians last year. He was pretty chummy with the Reds, even had a KGB major for a houseguest. We figure Ram might be a Commie, but he hasn't broken any laws...at least none that we can prove."

"Does the NSA still have anyone watching Ram's estate?" Calvin James asked.

"After the Russians vanished we figured they might have headed for Ram's place," Hislaw recalled. "We were watching him like hungry hawks after that. We put a tap on his phone, had a twenty-four-hour watch on the place, heat-sensing telescopes, radio microphones and everything else we could get our hands on was used to check on the son of a bitch. But Ram didn't have any Commie spies hiding out at his estate. We figured it was probably another phase the brat was going through. His old man has always been a capitalist who still does business with the British, so Ram might have just played games with the Russians to give the maharaja a bigger ulcer. NSA hasn't kept regular surveillance on Ram for the last four or five months. Maybe we should have."

"The situation requires more than that," Katz commented thoughtfully. "What kind of security does Ram have?"

"He's got about two dozen bodyguards stationed at his estate," the NSA man replied. "Strong-arm types. Back in the States guys like them are breaking legs for loan sharks. Now most of them carry guns, old British revolvers and side-by-side shotguns. Some of them might have rifles, but no automatic weapons unless they've kept the heavy-duty stuff hidden."

"What about alarms and electric eyes?" Encizo inquired. "Does Ram have closed-circuit television cameras or heat sensors set up around his estate?"

"Hell, no," Hislaw said. "This is India, man. Hardly anybody puts money into that kind of gadget except us. Besides, you guys aren't planning to attack Ram's place, are you?"

"It's possible," Katz said with a shrug. "But we'd rather just talk to him, providing he answers some questions and convinces us he's telling the truth."

"Well," Hislaw began awkwardly, "how do you plan to arrange a meeting with the prince? Sure, the royalty in India are just figureheads now; they have a lot of ceremony, but no real authority. Still, you can't just knock on his door and ask to see the prince."

"Why not?" McCarter asked with a grin. "We'll try not to pick our noses in the presence of his lordship."

"Are these guys nuts?" Hislaw asked, turning toward Lieutenant Tagore for an answer.

"I believe so, yes," the CID officer replied with a nod.

RAJPUT RAM SOMNOKA'S ESTATE was located to the north, about two hundred kilometers from Ranigan. The terrain was a bit rugged, but Phoenix Force had rented two Toyota Land Rovers that handled the task with ease. Tagore and Robert Hislaw accompanied the commando unit as the jeeps crept along the crude dirt road that bisected a bamboo forest. They heard numerous birds chirping and cawing among the slender trees.

"Jesus," Calvin James rasped, pointing at three struggling shapes among the bamboo. "Look at that."

Two large colorful birds were fighting with a snake. The birds resembled toucans with horny fins atop their beaks. They had pinned down the long scaly body of the reptile. The snake raised its head and spread a wide hood at its neck. The birds were not impressed. A beak snapped shut on the cobra's neck, nearly biting its head off.

"Hornbills," Lieutenant Tagore declared as he watched the birds tear the snake apart. "They're omnivorous and generally favor fruit and such to tangling with cobras.''

"Looks like they're doing a pretty good job," McCarter commented. ''Must have studied under a mongoose.''

"When hornbills hunt in pairs," Tagore explained, ''one distracts the prey and the other attacks. Then both finish off their opponent. Interesting strategy, eh?''

"Are there many snakes around here?" James asked with a frown. The black commando was not terrified of snakes, but would not mind if he never saw one again, either.

"A few," Hislaw answered. "But you don't have to worry about them as long as you're in the jeep."

"Wonderful," James muttered.

"What about tigers?" Encizo asked, more curious than concerned. ''This is the Bengal area, so maybe there are some Bengal tigers around.''

"Not very likely in a skimpy little forest like this," Tagore told him. "Tigers generally remain in dense tropical rain forests. Besides, there are probably only a few thousand tigers left in India. They're protected by law from hunters, but the forests are slowly vanishing, and the big cats are disappearing at the same time."

"I just hope you guys know what you're doing, or all of us might be on the endangered-species list," Hislaw muttered, turning the steering wheel to guide a Land Rover around a cluster of bamboo stalks. "We're approaching Prince Ram's estate."

An iron picket fence surrounded Rajput Somnoke's property. His palace was an odd combination of British and Islamic architecture with a European frame and a tear-shaped dome on the roof. The building was small for a palace, about the size of an English mansion. Four sentries patrolled the lawns behind the fence, all armed with Sterling submachine guns.

"I thought these blokes were suppose to be packing double-barreled shotguns," McCarter whispered sourly.

"Somebody decided they needed a little extra firepower," Manning replied. "Funny they should make that decision just before we show up. You don't suppose they're expecting us, do you?"

"Coincidences happen from time to time," Katz said, reaching for his briefcase. "But we'd better be ready in case this turns out to be more than that."

The Israeli called to Hislaw and told him to stop the lead jeep. They parked both vehicles about fifty yards from the front gate. The sentries watched them suspiciously as Katz climbed from a Land Rover and gestured to the others to stay put.

"I want most of you men to remain outside," the Phoenix Force commander instructed. "If they decide to attack, I don't want it to be easy for them to get all of us in a cross fire. Mr. Smythe, you like to work at close range."

"It's what I live for, Mr. Jacobs," McCarter replied with a grin.

"Then you'll accompany me," the Israeli declared. "I'll also need a translator in case Prince Ram doesn't speak English or he starts giving instructions to his men in a language I don't understand."

"I'll go with you," Hislaw said with a sigh. "I'm the logical choice because I speak Hindi, Urdu and Bengali—the local dialect of this region."

"I'd like to go in with you," Encizo announced. "I do my best work up close, too."

"All right," Katz agreed. "But the rest of you will stay out here. Now don't jump to conclusions. We don't know that Ram Somnoka is guilty of anything worse than bad taste in the company he chooses to keep. But don't fall asleep out here."

"Don't worry," Calvin James assured him. "Wouldn't want to miss the fun."

Katz, McCarter, Encizo and Hislaw approached the gate. The guards simply glared at them, hands poised by the triggers of their Sterling subguns. Yakov smiled at the sentries. He wore a white linen jacket and trousers and a white Panama hat. The Israeli appeared to be a European businessman, unless one noticed the bulge of the SIG-Sauer pistol holstered under his right arm. This was not terribly suspicious since many travelers in West Bengal carry weapons.

McCarter and Encizo both wore bush shirts and khaki trousers with paratrooper boots. They did not try to conceal the pistols holstered on their hips, although both men carried backup guns hidden in pancake holsters at the small of the back under their shirts. Encizo's Cold Steel Tanto knife was visible on his belt, but his Gerber Mk I dagger was in an ankle sheath beneath his pant leg. Hislaw also carried a pistol in a button-flap holster on his hip. The three Phoenix Force members held rather battered but innocent-looking attaché cases.

"Good afternoon," Katz greeted. "We'd like to talk to Rajput Ram Somnoka. Is the prince able to receive visitors?"

The sentries seemed confused. One of them spoke into a walkie-talkie. Hislaw asked the same question in Hindi and began to repeat it in Bengali, but a guard cut him off with a wave of the hand.

"We understand what you want," the sentry assured him, speaking English with a slight British accent. "Wait a moment, please. We will learn if our master will agree to see you gentlemen.''

"Don't you want to know who we are first?'' Rafael Encizo inquired.

"We know who you are,'' the guard told him. "You are from the American Embassy, yes? Or perhaps you are Interpol or NATO security agents. It makes no difference. You are Westerners, so your reason for being here will be much the same. All you Westerners are alike.''

"You've obviously never seen a political debate on the BBC,'' McCarter said dryly.

A static-laced voice on the walkie-talkie issued a curt order to the guards. The sentries exchanged nods and opened the gate. Manning and James, who remained by the Land Rovers, noticed the gate was not locked.

"You may enter,'' the English-speaking guard declared. "Rajput Ram Somnoka will see you.''

"Thank you,'' Katz replied as he led his four-man group across the threshold.

A sentry escorted them to the front door. A small, rat-faced man greeted them at the entrance. The ornate bronze handles of three knives jutted from a yellow sash around his thin waist, but he pressed his palms together at his chest and bowed humbly.

"Welcome, gentlemen,'' Kosti, the psycho killer priest of the Thuggees said with a smile. "Prince Ram is delighted to have such honored visitors in his home. Please follow me and I shall take you to him.''

Said the spider to the fly, Yakov Katzenelenbogen thought as he entered the palace of Rajput Somnoka.

14

Kosti led the four visitors into a handsome hallway with a black-and-white checkerboard floor and white-washed walls. Brass urns stood in the corners, and a long white marble staircase extended to the second story. Beautiful oil paintings hung on the walls. Most were eighteenth-century Indian art featuring maharajas on horseback or atop elephants with bejeweled tusks. Katz recognized the blue-skinned face of Lord Krishna in one painting. A favorite character of Indian artists, Krishna appeared to be courting a woman dressed in silk and seated upon a pile of large pillows.

"Hello, gentlemen," a voice greeted. "I am Ram Somnoka."

A young, slender man dressed in a long silk jacket with a Nehru collar welcomed the three Phoenix Force members and their NSA ally. A golden turban decorated the rajput's sleek head and several strings of black and yellow beads hung from his neck. Somnoka's right hand rested on the bronze haft of a scimitar. The sword remained in its scabbard as Somnoka used it as a walking stick.

"A great pleasure to meet you, sir," Katz replied, approaching the prince. "I apologize for coming here unannounced, and I hope our visit does not find you at an awkward time."

"Not at all," Ram Somnoka assured him. "And I must apologize for my guards. They can be a bit gruff at times."

"No problem," Encizo told him. "We're used to that sort of thing."

"Well," the rajput began, looking at the Cuban's sidearm with disdain, "my men were probably a bit disturbed by those guns."

"This is quite a distance from any towns or cities, Rajput Ram," Robert Hislaw stated. "One can't be too careful with bands of robbers roving about and dangerous animals that might wander from the rain forest. In fact, we saw a cobra on our way here."

"It has been my experience that robbers and wild beasts spend most of their time in the cities," Ram said with a smile. "No matter. Please follow me to the drawing room and we'll have some tea while we discuss whatever it is you people have on your minds."

Somnoka led them to a pair of wooden doors at the end of the hall. The rajput slid the doors open and prepared to step into the drawing room. Suddenly Somnoka dashed inside and ran to the cover of a large wing chair.

"Down!" Katz shouted as he jumped away from the door, left hand streaking for the SIG-Sauer autoloader under his arm.

McCarter instantly leaped to the opposite side of the door. Encizo swept an arm into Hislaw and threw himself backward. Both men flattened their backs against a wall. A monstrous roar exploded from the drawing room and a great swarm of lead pellets sizzled through the doorway. Several small projectiles tugged at Encizo's shirt, tearing cloth. A pellet stung flesh as it creased the Cuban's chest.

Kosti was less fortunate. The Thuggee priest had ventured too far into the hall, hoping to get a good view of the intended shotgun ambush. The sadist shrieked when buckshot smashed into his upper chest and face. The impact hurled Kosti to the floor, blood dripping from torn flesh.

Katz and McCarter drew their pistols and fired into the drawing room. The first three or four rounds were just to keep the shotgunners' heads down long enough for the Phoenix commandos to glance inside. They spotted three gunmen. The assailants instinctively ducked, but they fumbled with their shotguns and tried to fire another volley of buckshot.

McCarter had a clear target. The British pistol champ snap-aimed his Browning Hi-Power and squeezed off two shots. A 9mm slug smashed into the side of a shotgunner's jaw, shattering bone and slicing his tongue in half. The other bullet punched through the guy's skull, just below the right temple. The deadly 115-grain messenger burned into the flunky's brain and retired him from life—permanently.

Katz trained his SIG-Sauer P-226 on another shotgun killer and triggered his pistol. A parabellum round struck the ambusher in the upper torso, and the man's body jerked from the impact, his double-barrel blaster slipping from his grasp. Katz quickly fired two more shots. Both 9mm slugs slammed into the center of the bastard's chest. His heart and lungs were pulverized. The enemy henchman collapsed to the Persian carpet, blood oozing from his bullet-riddled corpse.

Encizo had popped open his briefcase and removed his MP-5 machine pistol. The Cuban worked the bolt to chamber the first round, then swung the Heckler & Koch chatterbox toward the drawing room and bent his knees to assume a crouch.

"Cover me!" Encizo shouted as he sprang forward.

Katz and McCarter continued to fire their pistols at the remaining shotgunner. They aimed high, trying to keep the enemy off balance without risking Encizo's life. The Cuban dived across the threshold, his body low and right shoulder canted forward.

Encizo hit the carpet, tumbled on his back and raised the MP-5. The shotgun hit man rose from behind a teakwood desk, his buckshot cannon in his fists. Encizo triggered his H&K machine pistol. A 3-round burst hit the gunman before he could fire his shotgun. Two 9mm slugs ripped open the hoodlum's throat, and the third ricocheted off the steel barrel of the guy's scatter-gun and flew into his face. By a freak chance, the parabellum round traveled straight up a nostril, sizzled through the sinus cavity and split bone to drill into the guy's brain.

The third shotgunner slumped behind the desk in a lifeless lump. Encizo began to rise, his MP-5 held ready. Suddenly Rajput Ram Somnoka appeared from behind the wing chair. The prince held his scimitar in both fists and raised the naked blade overhead. Encizo tried to swing his H&K blaster at Somnoka, but the Indian slashed his sword at the same instant. The long blade clanged against the frame of the Cuban's weapon, the blow wipping the MP-5 out of Encizo's grasp.

The gun fell to the floor as Ram Somnoka swung a backhand sword sweep at the Cuban's head. Encizo ducked beneath the whistling blade. The sharp steel brushed his hair, sending icy shards of fear along the Cuban's spine. Encizo was too experienced to freeze up. He charged forward and slammed into Ram before the prince could swing his sword again.

Encizo's left hand snared Somnoka's sleeve as he punched his right fist under the Indian's ribs. The Phoenix Force hardass followed through with a solid right cross to Ram's jaw. The rajput groaned as his head bounced from the punch, but he responded by thrusting the tip of his scimitar at Encizo's stomach.

Encizo sidestepped the stabbing blade and grabbed his opponent's wrist. He yanked Somnoka's arm downward and slammed it across his knee. The rajput's hand popped open and the scimitar dropped to the floor. Encizo quickly rammed an elbow to Somnoka's breastbone and whipped a backfist to the prince's face.

Somnoka fell back against a wall, blood trickling from his mouth and nose. Suddenly Ram lashed out a leg and kicked a slipper-clad foot into Encizo's abdomen. The Cuban gasped and folded slightly at the waist. Somnoka slammed his left fist into Encizo's face, knocking the Phoenix warrior two feet backward.

The rajput bent over to retrieve his scimitar, and as Somnoka's fist closed around the handle of his sword, Encizo stamped a boot on the blade and pinned it to the floor. The Cuban smiled at the prince and suddenly kicked him in the face. Somnoka sprawled on his back as Encizo kicked the sword across the room.

"I think you've had it, your highness," the Cuban said.

Ram Somnoka sat up, mopping his crushed mouth with the back of a hand. He spat out a rude remark in Hindi and crawled toward the H&K MP-5. Encizo reached for the Smith & Wesson 9mm pistol on his hip, but he did not draw the gun. He wanted Somnoka alive. The Cuban's hand streaked to his belt buckle and yanked a *shaken* throwing star from the brass base. Encizo hurled the weapon. Somnoka screamed when a sharp metal point pierced his triceps. The prince rolled over on his back, clawing at the star-shaped projectile lodged in his upper arm.

"Okay, *chico*," Encizo sighed, drawing his pistol. "Try that again and we'll have a royal funeral."

THE SOUNDS OF THE GUN BATTLE alerted Manning, James and Lieutenant Tagore that it was time to go into action. Calvin James drew an M-16 assault rifle from his duffel bag. An M-203 grenade launcher was attached to the bottom of the barrel and a banana-shaped 50-round extended magazine was fitted into the well above the trigger guard. Lieutenant Tagore reached inside a Land Rover for his Sterling Mk IV submachine gun while Manning opened another duffel bag to get his Remington shotgun and other gear.

"Halt!" one of the palace guards shouted as he stuck the barrel of his subgun between the iron bars of the fence.

Two other sentries also aimed their weapons at the Phoenix Force duo and their CID companion. But none of them got a chance to open fire. Calvin James suddenly swung his M-16 at the closest guard and squeezed the trigger. A 3-round volley of 5.56mm hail tore into the guy's face, chopping his features into crimson slime and blasting his skull apart.

Tagore fired his Sterling, hosing the gate with 9mm slugs. Sparks appeared as bullets ricocheted off iron pickets. A sentry screamed when other parabellums slammed into his chest and punctured the hollow of his throat. The guard slid down the length of the gate as one of his comrades tried to train a subgun on the CID lieutenant.

James's M-16 spat fire once more. Three 5.56mm
slugs tore into the sentry's left deltoid. The impact spun
the gunman around to receive another trio of high-
velocity rifle rounds between the shoulder blades. The
guy fell face first on the lawn, his spinal cord severed and
both lungs torn to shreds.

Gary Manning slid behind the wheel of the first jeep.
He placed the Remington shotgun on the seat beside him
and drew his .357 Colt Magnum from shoulder leather.
James and Tagore climbed in the back seat as Manning
started the engine.

The Canadian stomped on the gas pedal, and the Land
Rover charged forward like an angry bull. It crashed into
the front gate, slamming open the unlocked barrier.
Tires rolled over the corpse of a slain sentry. The jeep
hardly bounced as it crushed the body into the ground.

More members of Prince Somnoka's security force
immediately appeared. Gunmen charged across the
lawn, armed with an assortment of submachine guns,
shotguns and pistols. Snipers aimed weapons from the
second-story windows, and one gunman appeared along
the cornice of the roof.

Calvin James raised his M-16 and fired back at the
second-story snipers while Tagore hosed the foot soldiers with 9mm slugs. A burst of 5.56mm rounds picked
off a rifleman armed with an old Enfield rifle. The man
screamed as he tumbled over the windowsill and plunged
to the ground below. Two guards hopped and jerked in
a spasm of death as Tagore blasted them with his Sterling subgun.

Manning turned the steering wheel sharply to the left
and spun the jeep across the lawn. The Canadian spotted a gunman in a kneeling stance who was trying to aim
a shotgun at the windshield of the Land Rover. Man-

ning extended his left arm, the Colt Magnum in his fist. He triggered the revolver twice, his brawny arm easily absorbing the recoil of the big .357 Mag.

Two powerful high-velocity .357 projectiles punched through the guard's body as if he were made of tissue paper. He fell backward as he pulled a trigger to his double-barrel blast machine. The shotgun roared, spewing buckshot at the sky above.

James shot another sniper at the second story. He saw the man recoil from a window to clamp both hands to his bullet-shattered face. The black warrior heard something slam into the backrest of the seat beside him. A rifle slug had pierced the upholstery a few inches from James's backside.

"You son of a bitch," James growled as he swung his M-16 toward the gunman stationed on the roof. "I'm gonna have your ass for that, man!"

He fired a 3-round volley at the sniper, but the guy had ducked behind the curved base of the tear-shaped dome. The M-16 slugs just bounced off the marble surface. The gunman's head poked around the edge, as if taunting James.

"Motherfucker," the black man snarled as he moved his finger to the trigger of the M-203 attachment.

The grenade launcher belched, the recoil driving the plastic stock of the M-16 painfully against James's hip. A 40mm projectile sailed to the roof. Heavy explosives erupted on contact with the dome, and the mangled body of the sniper was hurled from the roof as if propelled by a catapult.

Lieutenant Tagore blasted two more opponents with the last parabellums from his Sterling subgun. The gunmen fell to the ground in a twitching, dying collection of arms and legs as Tagore hastily swapped magazines.

Manning brought the Land Rover to a full halt. He holstered his Magnum and gathered up the Remington riot gun. James jumped from the back of the jeep and dropped into a crouch, placing the barrel of his M-16 across the frame of the vehicle for a bench rest.

More security guards dashed from the palace to attack the trio by the jeep. Snipers continued to fire at them from the second-story windows. Tagore jumped down beside James, also using the Land Rover for cover. The black fighting machine squeezed off several rounds at the troops below. Two more enemies cried out and dropped to the ground with 5.56mm lead poisoning. The others threw themselves flat and adopted prone positions to fire back at Manning, James and Tagore.

"Hey, man," James called to Manning, "you got anything in your bag of tricks to help us outta this mess?"

"Yeah," the Canadian demolitions expert replied as he took a plastic disk, similar to a Frisbee, from a canvas sack. "Let's play a little catch with these guys."

Manning adjusted a dial in the center of the disk and hurled it. The saucer spun across the lawn and whistled over the heads of the prone guard force. The timer detonated six ounces of C-4 plastic explosives. The disk burst into a miniature supernova that blasted a massive hole in the lawn and tore the gunmen apart like insects trapped in an electric blender.

Only two enemies on the ground survived. Both men were wounded. As they crawled awkwardly to their feet and tried to limp to safety, Lieutenant Tagore cut them down with a volley of 9mm slugs.

Calvin James fired his M-16 at the snipers while Manning set the timer of another C-4 Frisbee. The Canadian threw the disk in a long, high arch. It spun through the air and whirled straight for the second-story windows. The plastic saucer exploded. One sniper was literally decapitated by the blast. His headless body plunged to the ground, blood squirting from the ragged stump of his neck.

Chopera, the muscle-bound subpriest of the Thuggees also fell from a second-story window, jarred over the sill by the violent vibrations caused by the explosion. Chopera crashed into a row of bushes at the base of the house. The hedge broke his fall and saved the brute from a bone-breaking encounter with the ground.

With the security force soundly defeated, James and Tagore dashed for the door of the palace. Manning slipped the strap of his bag over a shoulder, gathered up his Remington and ran after his partners. Chopera leaped from the bushes and dived into the Canadian.

Both men fell to the ground. Manning's shotgun was knocked from his grasp, but the Canadian slashed a karate chop to Chopera's face. The Indian's head recoiled from the blow, blood oozing from a split lip. Manning rose to his feet and reached for his .357 revolver.

Chopera's left hand seized Manning's arm and stopped him from drawing the Magnum. The big Indian's right fist slammed into the Canadian, and Manning gasped and doubled up from the force of the punch. Chopera quickly wrapped his left arm around Manning's neck and raised his fist. A cestus made of buffalo horn covered the knuckles. The *vajra-musti* knuckle duster is potentially lethal, especially in the fist of a muscular killer like Chopera.

The Indian's cestus-clad fist rocketed for Manning's face. The Canadian was still held fast by Chopera's headlock, but both his arms were free. Manning's left hand deflected Chopera's punch with a heel-of-the-palm parry. His right delivered a karate ridge-hand stroke between Chopera's legs. The Indian killer wheezed in pain when Manning used his testicles for a volleyball. The Phoenix Force commando pried the guy's arm from his neck, but Chopera immediately swung a deadly right cross at Manning's head.

As the Canadian weaved and stepped forward, the cestus fist whistled past his left ear. Manning grabbed Chopera's arm and pivoted. He bent his knees and jammed his shoulder into the Indian's armpit. Manning hauled the big man off his feet and hurled him to the ground with a judo shoulder throw.

Chopera broke his fall by slapping an arm to the ground to absorb most of the impact. The Indian's legs suddenly shot up, and his ankles snapped a scissors hold around Manning's neck. Chopera twisted his body and threw the Canadian head over heels to the ground. Then the Indian raised a foot to stomp Manning's face to pulp.

The Canadian warrior moved his head aside, and Chopera's heel stamped a rut in the ground. Manning rolled away from his opponent and leaped to his feet. Chopera tried to rise, but he was a tad too slow. Manning stepped in and rammed his fist into the Indian's face. Chopera fell on all fours. The Canadian kicked the guy in the ribs and clasped his hands together to chop them at the base of Chopera's neck.

The big Indian fell on his face, only dazed by a blow that would have killed an ordinary man. Manning dropped on Chopera's back, planting a knee at the small of his opponent's spine. Chopera groaned and tried to buck the commando off, but Manning scooped both hands under the Indian's chin and interlaced the fingers.

Chopera knew what was about to happen. He desperately reached for Manning's fingers to try to break the hold under his jaw. The Canadian did not hesitate. He hauled back forcibly. The ugly crack of breaking vertebrae rewarded Manning's efforts. Chopera's body fell limp. Manning released him and rose to his feet. He had broken the Indian's back.

INSIDE THE PALACE, Yakov Katzenelenbogen and David McCarter also had their hands full. While Encizo was busy subduing Prince Somnoka, two gunmen appeared on the stairwell overlooking the hall. The pair prepared to aim their weapons at the Israeli commando.

Katz whirled, his SIG-Sauer braced across his prosthesis. The Phoenix Force commander fired three rapid shots at the gunmen. One 9mm round splintered wood from the handrail, but the other two crashed into the chest of one of the ambushers. The triggerman cried out and tumbled down the marble staircase. The other gunman quickly retreated back up the stairs.

McCarter had taken his Ingram M-10 from a briefcase. He glanced into the drawing room and saw Encizo binding Ram Somnoka's wrists behind his back with plastic riot cuffs. Robert Hislaw was unaccustomed to being in the middle of a firefight, but his hands were steady when he finally drew his Government Issue Colt .45 from its holster.

Another door in the hall burst open and three gunmen charged from a dining room. McCarter instantly opened fire with his machine pistol. One of the goons was thrown back into the room by the force of three parabellums in the chest. Another flunky doubled up with 9mm rounds in the gut. The third dived to the floor and tried to train his Sterling subgun on the Briton. Hislaw's

.45 bellowed and a big 230 solid-ball projectile smashed through the gunman's forehead. The NSA case officer's mouth fell open as he stared at the puddle of blood and brains that leaked from the man's shattered skull.

"Thanks, mate," McCarter told him, aiming his Ingram at the wounded gunman who was trying to push his intestines back inside his belly.

The Briton hosed the guy with another burst of full-auto destruction and ended his suffering forever. Katz had removed his Uzi from his valise and slid the SIG-Sauer into shoulder leather. He turned to Hislaw.

"Shout in Hindi to let these morons know we'll take prisoners if any of them have enough sense to surrender," Katz told the NSA man.

"I can do better than that," Encizo announced as he shoved Prince Somnoka into the hall. "His royal highness is going to order his men to stop their attack or I'll blow his brains out."

Ram Somnoka cried out to his men, shouting commands in Hindi and Bengali. Calvin James and Lieutenant Tagore entered the building as the rajput completed ordering the guard force to surrender. Two men descended the stairs, their empty hands held high. Three more henchmen approached from the dining room, their arms raised with hands over head.

"You see what can be accomplished with a little co-operation?" Katz commented.

15

Katz, James and Tagore questioned Rajput Ram Somnoka while the other members of the assault force took care of the prisoners and checked the palace to be certain no die-hard defenders were preparing a sneak attack. James, the Phoenix Force medic, cleaned and bandaged the *shaken* wound in the prince's upper arm. Katz offered Somnoka a cigarette. The rajput refused, so Katz fired it up for himself.

"All right, Prince Ram," the Israeli began, blowing smoke through his nostrils, "we came here to find out what you can tell us about the KGB and the Cult of Kali. If we needed any evidence that you're involved in something shady, you certainly supplied us with it when you tried to kill us."

"That's your word against mine," Somnoka replied, gritting his teeth as James knotted the bandage on his arm. "I am, after all, a member of the Indian nobility."

"This is the twentieth century, man," James said dryly. "Your title doesn't mean a hell of a lot anymore. You don't have any real authority, but you're messin' with some people who do."

"You see," Katz continued, "we're acting with the approval of both the governments of India and the United States of America. This means we can kill you right now if we want or place you under arrest for conspiracy to commit murder, espionage against your own country and probably as an accomplice to murder, as well."

"You can't prove anything," Somnoka insisted. "You bastards attacked my palace, and my men acted in self-defense."

"Your reputation isn't exactly pure, Ram," Katz said. "Your word won't mean much in court, especially after we introduce evidence that you were cooperating with several members of the Soviet embassy, including a man who has been positively identified as a major in the KGB. If we don't have enough evidence to make certain you get convicted, we'll simply fabricate as much as we need."

"You bastards," Somnoka shouted.

Katz suddenly swatted the back of his left hand across Ram's face. The prince yelped from the unexpected pain and stared at Yakov, astonished that the Israeli had struck him.

"Listen to me, you little creep," Katz said in a grim voice, his expression as hard as diamonds. "You're part of a conspiracy that has been killing innocent people and trying to set the groundwork for an eventual overthrow of your own country by the Soviet Union. Most of the Thuggees are probably ignorant, frightened and uneducated recruits from the peasant classes. They'd be easy victims for a clever con artist with some Russian technology to make the tricks more convincing."

"I don't know what you're talking about," Somnoka told him.

"We know what the Soviets have been doing," Katz said, deciding to use some of his own assumptions and theories to try to bluff Somnoka. "We know about the mechanical statue of Kali with a built-in laser cannon."

"How…" the prince began, "uh, would such a statue be connected with this wild claim about a conspiracy?"

"The hell with this dude," James said. "He's a murderer and a traitor to his own country. He can't even plead ignorance like those poor fanatics we tangled with in Bombay. Princey and his boys didn't try to take us on with just silk cords."

"What are you going to do?" Tagore asked. "Give him a dose of truth serum?"

"Might kill him," James replied with a shrug. "But I don't care if it does. Anybody else give a damn?"

"Wait!" Somnoka exclaimed. "If I cooperate, how do I know you won't kill me?"

"We're professionals," Katz answered. "We don't kill people unless there's a very good reason. If you can supply us with information about the Thugs and the KGB, we have no reason to kill you and a good reason to keep you alive."

"Will I have to stand trial?" Prince Ram asked. "Will I have to go to prison?"

"That'll depend on how cooperative you are," Katz told him. "Frankly you'll have to prove to be very valuable to convince us that you shouldn't spend some time behind bars."

"Personally," James muttered, "I figure you're the worst kind of low-life. A dude who has a silver spoon in his mouth since birth can't even use the feeble excuse that he needed bread or he was trying to liberate his oppressed people so he teamed up with the Commies. What is your excuse, anyway? Did the Reds just offer you enough money to buy your loyalty?"

"The Russians promised me West Bengal," Somnoka replied. "They said it would be mine to rule as an independent state. I could rule it as a true maharaja, with the support of the Soviets, but without their direct control."

"Major Yousopov told you that, I suppose," Yakov said dryly. "He's the KGB control officer you had for a houseguest. Did Yousopov tell you what he was doing in Afghanistan a while back? He wasn't helping them establish self-rule."

"Where is the headquarters of the Cult of Kali?" Lieutenant Tagore demanded. "You've tried to betray our country, Somnoka, so you'd better..."

Tagore suddenly stiffened, his face contorted with pain. He opened his mouth and blood streamed over his lips. The CID man stumbled forward and fell to the floor, the hilt of a brass-handled dagger jutting from his back.

James and Katz turned to face the assailant. Kosti stood in the hallway, leaning against a wall. His face and chest had been torn and bloodied by buckshot pellets, but the psycho Thuggee priest had survived the blast he had received during the gun battle. Kosti still smiled, although half his face looked like fresh hamburger, dripping crimson. The lunatic raised another dagger and prepared to throw it.

Calvin James drew his Colt Commander and thumbed off the safety catch. He aimed the weapon swiftly and squeezed the trigger. The pistol roared and the recoil raised the black man's arm toward the ceiling. A .45-caliber projectile bashed through Kosti's chest and smashed his sternum to bits. The impact sent the homicidal priest sliding along the length of the wall. James shot him again, pumping a second 185-grain hollow-point slug into the bastard's chest.

Katz unleashed his SIG-Sauer autoloader and fired two 9mm rounds into Kosti before the murderous

Thuggee leader hit the floor. James knelt by the fallen body of Lieutenant Tagore as Katz marched to Kosti's inert form and shot him in the back of the skull to make certain the son of a bitch stayed dead.

"Oh, shit!" Calvin James rasped in frustrated anger. "The knife got Tagore under the left shoulder blade. He's dead. Blade slid right into his heart."

"At least it was quick," Katz said softly, shoving his SIG-Sauer into shoulder leather.

"Guess what, Somnoka?" James snarled, pointing the bloodied tip of the killer dagger at the prince's face. "This doesn't exactly put us in a good mood, man. You'd better not fuck around with us if you wanta stay in one piece."

"I'll tell you where to find the mountain of Kali," Somnoka said quickly, fearful for his life.

"You'll do better than that, Prince Ram," Katz told him. "You're going to take us there."

16

The Benares mountain range is not very impressive compared to the Himalayas located to the north at Nepal. In fact, they're rather puny compared to the Alps or the Rockies. The Benares extend across the Bihar region to the outskirts of the Madhya Pradesh. The terrain is basically rocky and hard with patches of green. Few trees grow in the Benares range, mostly weeds and thistles. The environment is not hospitable to any form of life, including human.

Phoenix Force, accompanied by Robert Hislaw and a highly unnerved Prince Ram Somnoka, arrived at the Benares a few hours after sunup. The area was too rugged even for the jeeps, so they were forced to abandon the Land Rovers and continue on foot.

"I've got a question for his royal hind end before we go any farther," Rafael Encizo declared, turning toward Somnoka. "Several of the Thugs we questioned claimed they were blindfolded and transported to the mountain of Kali in a truck. If this is the right place, how do the trucks get to the mountain?"

"They have to get out of the trucks and walk," Somnoka answered. His right arm was in a sling, and he cradled it with his left. "They're still blindfolded, linked together by a rope and led by Kosti or Chopera or one of my men."

"Who are Kosti and Chopera?" Hislaw inquired.

"They were two of the subpriests of Kali," the rajput explained. "You don't have to worry about them anymore. They were both killed back at my palace. May the gods curse their souls for a thousand incarnations."

"You mad at them because they got killed?" James asked, sliding the strap of his M-16 onto a shoulder.

"Those two had been sent to set up an ambush at my palace in case your group came," Somnoka admitted. "They brought those British submachine guns, purchased from some gunrunner for such an occasion. Yousopov didn't want Soviet-made weapons to be used in case something went wrong. Chopera and Kosti were so smug, so certain they could lure your group into a trap. Of course, those fools failed."

"Forgive us if we don't get too upset about that," Gary Manning commented. "How many Thugs and Russians are probably waiting for us at Kali mountain?"

"I don't know," the prince admitted. "Perhaps thirty. Perhaps two hundred or more. I don't know how many Russian soldiers are under Yousopov's command or how many Thuggees are members of Nangal's cult."

"Okay," James said, "who the hell is Nangal?"

"He's the supreme high priest of the Thuggees," the rajput stated. "Nangal is a fake prophet who has formed false cults before. He's a clever speaker and knows how to get his followers to believe the most outrageous claims. The Russians could never have succeeded with the Thuggee scheme without him."

"Well, gentlemen," Katz remarked, gazing up at the peaks of the Benares set against the pink and gold morning sky, "we'd better prepare for the worst. The odds will certainly be in the enemy's favor. Perhaps even forty to one."

"Jesus," Hislaw muttered, "I wish we'd contacted the Indian CID or the military for reinforcements. This is crazy, and I've gotta be nuts to go along with you guys."

"We already told you why we couldn't call in reinforcements from the CID or the Indian military," McCarter replied. "The Thuggees had at least one agent in the CID. We knew we could trust Lieutenant Tagore because he proved to be reliable when we hit the Bhowani temple in Bombay, but we can't be sure about anybody else CID might send. The army has probably been infiltrated by Thuggees, as well. By the time we could select some men we could trust, the KGB would have closed up shop and taken the Thuggees underground until they were ready to start business somewhere else."

"Mr. Smythe is right," Katz said, referring to McCarter by his cover name. "When they figure out the ambush at Ram's palace failed, they'll realize it's time to stop operations until the heat cools off. We can't allow them enough time to fold up their tents and steal off unmolested."

"These mountains are dangerous," Somnoka warned. "Bahir Khan and his bandits roam the area. They're a dangerous lot. Bahir Khan is a wild man from the Mongolian tribes to the north. He is clever and very ruthless. His men are an assortment of misfits. Most are Moslem radicals, anarchists who once fought to overthrow the Indian government that they believe oppresses non-Hindus. Now they fight only for profit."

"Mercenaries?" Encizo inquired.

"The worst kind of mercenaries," Somnoka confirmed. "Major Yousopov pays Bahir Khan to leave the Thuggees alone. The bandits also serve as a first line of defense for the cult in case enemies get too close to their stronghold."

"That's nice," McCarter commented. "I didn't think we had enough to worry about with just the Thuggees and the KGB to deal with. Any idea how many bandits this Bahir Khan chap has in his outfit?"

"At least forty men," Somnoka replied. "And every one of them is a cold-blooded killer. They know these mountains like a man knows his wife's breasts. Bahir Khan and his killers can strike from anywhere, anytime."

"Well," Katz said with a shrug, "the situation isn't going to improve by wasting time talking about it. Let's get to work."

Phoenix Force was certainly ready for work. They wore brown-and-green camouflage uniforms. James wore the "tiger stripe" camies favored by the SEALs in Vietnam, and McCarter wore a sand-colored SAS beret with a winged-dagger badge. All five men carried their chosen weapons and plenty of ammunition. They had backpacks loaded with ropes and grappling hooks as well as smoke grenades and first-aid equipment. Naturally James carried additional medical supplies, and Manning had plenty of explosives.

Robert Hislaw was armed with a Sterling submachine gun and spare ammo taken from slain opponents at Ram Somnoka's palace. The NSA man was also equipped with his 1911 A-1 Colt pistol and a Marine Combat bowie. Somnoka was not armed, but he had not been manacled either. With a wounded arm, the rajput presented little threat to Phoenix Force. He was aware that any attempt to flee or assist the enemy would mean a swift execution.

The assault team began the long trek across the rugged terrain. Kali mountain was several miles away, according to Somnoka. They paced themselves carefully.

Exhausted men cannot perform at peak level, and they had to stay alert to possible ambush every step of the way.

Narrow gaps and bumpy passes ran between the gray stone mountains. Boulders lay in the path, and the great rocks slowed progress. They might also be a place of concealment for one or more bandits.

An hour after the journey began, the sun began to beat down on them like an open oven in the sky. Sweat ran freely from their pores leaving damp patches on their shirts under their arms and between their shoulder blades. The march was especially difficult for Hislaw, who was unaccustomed to such physical exertion. Ram Somnoka had made the journey before, so it was easier for the prince than one might have thought.

They had traveled almost four miles without incident. Then the sound of rocks sliding against a stone wall echoed among the mountains. A strange whinny sound followed, but ended abruptly. The Phoenix Force members immediately bolted for the nearest cover. Hislaw and Somnoka followed their example and huddled behind boulders with the commandos.

"Where the hell is the noise coming from?" Hislaw whispered, fumbling with his Sterling subgun. "Sounds like a horse—"

"Shut up," Encizo said sharply. "Keep your ears and eyes open and your mouth shut."

Something moved along the edge of a stone formation. The object was a mere blur of movement. Phoenix Force held fire and waited for a clear target. The sound of boot leather against stone rode the wind. It was impossible to tell where the noise came from. It probably came from more than one direction. Rock formations surrounded the assault force. Unseen adversaries could be anywhere and everywhere.

Without warning, rifle shots exploded from the rocks. Large-caliber bullets sang against the stone walls above Phoenix Force and ricocheted off the boulders they used for cover. All the commandos could see of their attackers was the muzzle-flash of their weapons. The gunmen were firing their rifles between boulders that offered ideal concealment.

More shots snarled from the peak of the rock formation above the shelter of Phoenix Force. McCarter raised his Ingram and fired up at the ambushers. Bullets sparked against rock, but at least one 9mm round struck a turbaned figure at the pinnacle of the stone tower. The man dropped his old Lee Enfield Mk VI and tumbled from his perch with a shriek.

Gary Manning had exchanged his Remington shotgun for an FN FAL rifle before heading for the Benares range. The Canadian warrior aimed his NATO assault piece at the boulders where the snipers were hidden. He peered through the Bushnell scope, but failed to find a clear target. Calvin James aimed his M-16 in the same direction. He didn't have any better luck than Manning.

"These guys are doing a good job at keeping their heads down," the Canadian growled.

"Could try to flush 'em out," James commented.

"I don't think they'd fall for it," Manning replied. "Probably just move to another position. Just wait..."

Two heads suddenly appeared above the boulders. Manning and James immediately opened fire. The skulls of the enemy gunmen exploded like a pair of balloons, splashing the rocks with blood and slimy gray brain matter.

More gunshots erupted from other boulders and rock formations. Hislaw fired a burst of Sterling slugs at two or more gunmen hidden behind a stony barrier. Bullets bounced off rock, but failed to strike flesh. The gunmen scrambled for new cover while other ambushers fired down from a rock formation higher up.

"Time to kick over the ant mound," James declared as he triggered the M-203 attachment on the barrel of his sixteen.

A 40mm grenade hurled against the rock hill, and the explosion blasted away half a ton of stone at the peak. Two bandit bodies were thrown into the sky, the corpses maimed and bloodied. More gunmen bolted from cover to avoid falling rock, and Encizo hosed them with full-auto 9mm rounds. Three bandits fell and convulsed in the final spasms of death.

Manning set the detonator of a plastic disk and spun it at the pinnacle of another rock formation. The C-4 loaded Frisbee exploded and another stony structure came tumbling down. Four bandits were scattered among the debris that tumbled into the gorge below.

Five outlaws suddenly rose at the pinnacle of a hill and began firing a concentrated stream of .303 rifle slugs at the Phoenix Force position. Bullets sang along the rock wall above their heads, but Katz ignored the near misses and raised his Uzi. The Israeli triggered a long salvo, drawing his full-auto fire across the figures on the summit. Two bandits screamed and fell from view. The other three hastily retreated.

The shooting stopped as abruptly as it had begun. Katz swapped magazines in his Uzi. James shoved a fresh cartridge grenade into the breech of his M-203. Manning opened his pack and removed a smoke grenade while McCarter selected an SAS flash-bang concussion grenade. Hislaw tried to count the number of bandits they had killed thus far.

"Don't waste time with a body count," Encizo told him, checking the magazine of his H&K MP-5 to be certain he did not run out of ammo. "There are still enough bastards left to attack us again."

"How do you figure they'll hit us next?" Hislaw asked, gripping the frame of his Sterling until his knuckles strained white against his skin.

"Well," McCarter replied as he hung a concussion grenade on his belt, "they tried to get us bottled in and shoot us. That didn't work so they'll try something else. If they aren't in a hurry, they may just wait for us to move and try to set up a better ambush later."

"They might try to rush us," Encizo commented, placing a smoke grenade on a stone ledge near his feet. "If they're mad enough and still have superior numbers, that'd be a logical tactic to try to drive us out in the open."

"Explosives would be better," Manning stated. "That's what I'd do. Lob a couple grenades or dynamite down on us. Either blow us to hell or drive us into the open."

"Maybe we're lucky and they don't have any explosives," James said. "They haven't used any so far."

"Anyone can make a simple grenade," the Canadian demolitions pro remarked. "Doesn't take much more than some gunpowder, a container and a fuse."

"Keep it down," Encizo said. "They might hear you."

"We can't stay here," Prince Ram Somnoka told the others. "Bahir Khan and his men will cut us to pieces."

"They can do that just as easily if we run out in the open," Katz replied. "Right now, everybody stay put and…"

Suddenly Somnoka scrambled over the boulder and ran into the open pass. He waved his uninjured arm and shouted in Hindi at the top of his lungs. McCarter swung his Ingram machine pistol at the prince, but Katz placed his hook on the barrel to restrain the Briton.

"Let him go," the Israeli said. "He can't tell the bandits anything they haven't already found out for themselves."

"Somnoka is telling the outlaws to hold their fire," Hislaw translated. "He's telling them who he is and that he's part of the Cult of Kali. He just added that the Russians want him protected."

Two rifles boomed from the rocks. Rajput Ram Somnoka stopped running when a pair of .303 slugs slammed into his chest. The prince half turned and fell to his knees. His face was a mask of astonishment as a trail of blood hung from his open mouth. Another rifle spoke and a bullet punched through Somnoka's back and burst a large exit wound in the center of his chest. The prince dropped on his face, too dead even to twitch.

"Looks like Bahir Khan and his boys weren't impressed," Manning said dryly.

Suddenly gunshots exploded from the rock walls, raining lead projectiles down on Phoenix Force. The commandos fired back at their opponents, although they saw little more than a few blurred figures among the stones. James unleashed another M-203 grenade and blasted at least three more bandits to the next world.

The thunder of horse hooves mingled with the roar of the explosion and the echo of gunshots. Four men on horseback charged the Phoenix shelter, accompanied by almost a dozen bandits on foot. The horsemen and foot soldiers attacked from both ends of the pass, hoping to catch Phoenix Force in a two-pronged attack while they were still pinned down by the sniper fire.

Manning and James continued to fire up at the gunmen on the rocks. Several snipers got careless, assuming Phoenix Force would be distracted by the ground attack. The gunmen rose to get a better target and exposed themselves to the two commando marksmen. James pumped ten 5.56mm rounds into two snipers while Manning shot down three bandits with his FN FAL rifle.

Katz and McCarter opened fire at one group of attacking bandits on horseback and on foot while Encizo and Hislaw defended their position from the other direction. Horses whinnied and toppled to the ground, throwing their riders. Outlaws cried out as full-auto bullets crashed into their flesh and crushed organs. Dead men and slain horses littered the ground, but more bandits immediately replaced them.

"Hasn't gotten rough enough for you blokes, eh?" McCarter rasped as he pulled the pin from his concussion grenade.

The Briton hurled the miniblaster, and the grenade exploded, creating a violent shock wave that hurled four bandits to the ground in a cluster of broken bones. Seven others fell screaming, clutching the sides of their heads as if trying to restore their shattered eardrums.

Encizo threw a smoke grenade as three more horsemen charged into the pass, firing revolvers and cut-down rifles as they rode. Thick columns of green fog suddenly spewed up at the bandits. Both horses and men were startled and disoriented by the tactic. The animals reared and bellowed in fear. Riders were pitched from their saddles. Bandits groped in the dense green smoke. Two men emerged from the dark cloud only to be gunned down by Encizo and Hislaw.

Then fate pulled a dirty trick. The wind changed suddenly and spread the smoke across the pass. The fog was not as thick, but it covered the Phoenix Force position as well as the bandits'. The snipers held their fire, unable to see well enough to know if they would be shooting at the commandos or their own men. Almost three dozen outlaws charged the Phoenix position, most armed with revolvers or knives.

Calvin James fired the last two rounds from his M-16 into the chest of a pistol-wielding outlaw. The bandit fell dead but a pair of small men, armed with large knives with long recurved blades, attacked. The pair were renegade Gurkhas from Nepal. The Gurkhas have a well-deserved reputation for being among the best fighting men in the world. They also have a religious tradition of not returning a *kukri* knife to its sheath until the blade has drawn blood. James was in no doubt about whose blood they intended to shed.

One Gurkha attempted an overhead stroke, swinging his knife like an executioner's ax. The other swung his *kukri* in a cross-body sweep. James raised his rifle to block the first blade with the barrel of his M-16, but the other knife caught the gun and yanked it out of the black man's hands.

James quickly lashed a tae kwon-do roundhouse kick to the guy's ribs. The Gurkha grunted, stumbled slightly and raised his knife. The other Gurkha tried to move around his partner to attack James from a different position. The black warrior concentrated on the immediate threat first. He dodged the *kukri* slash and pivoted, swinging the back of a heel into his opponent's breadbasket.

The Gurkha doubled up with a groan and Calvin quickly slashed a karate chop to the base of the man's neck. With a war cry, the second Gurkha charged, his *kukri* held in a two-fisted grip and drawn over his shoulder. James suddenly grabbed his first opponent by the back of his shirt and hurled the little warrior into his knife-wielding comrade.

The second Gurkha had already started his *kukri* stroke, and he could not stop it fast enough to spare his partner. The sharp, recurved blade struck the first Gurkha in the side of the neck, slicing through skin, muscle and bone. The first Gurkha's head hopped from the stump of his neck as blood spewed up from the grisly corpse.

James did not give the remaining Gurkha an opportunity to try again. He delivered a thrust kick to his adversary's arms. The side of his foot struck hard, knocking the *kukri* knife from the guy's hands. James followed through with a hook kick to the Gurkha's kidney and then snap-kicked him in the gut. The Gurkha staggered, dazed by the barrage of tae kwon-do kicks. James stepped forward and lashed a backfist across his opponent's face, followed by a left hook. The Gurkha dropped unconscious at Calvin's feet.

Rafael Encizo had shot down three charging bandits before his H&K machine pistol ran out of ammo. Another outlaw executed a wild knife lunge for the Cuban's belly, and Encizo sidestepped the clumsy attack and slammed the frame of his MP-5 against the guy's head. The man fell senseless, but another knife artist replaced him.

The guy was armed with a Bundi dagger, a unique and fearsome weapon with an H-shaped handle and a long double-edged blade. The Indian knife artist executed a rapid figure-eight stroke with his blade, forcing Encizo to back away fast.

The Cuban discarded his empty MP-5 and quickly drew his Cold Steel Tanto. The Bundi expert punched his dagger at Encizo's chest. The Tanto rose swiftly. Metal changed against metal as the Cold Steel blade parried the attack. Encizo punted a short side kick to his opponent's abdomen. The Bundi man staggered back two steps, but did not double up from the kick. He noticed the big combat knife in the Cuban's fist. The Indian smiled and nodded, apparently welcoming the challenge.

Encizo was less than thrilled by the contest, but he stood his ground and waited for the Bundi man to make the next move. The Indian hissed like a snake and made a weaving gesture with his knife. Encizo realized he was up against some sort of martial-arts technique, possibly *binot* style, modeled after a cobra. It did not fill him with confidence to be pitted against an opponent who used a fighting style he knew nothing about.

Suddenly the Indian lashed a kick at Encizo's genitals and struck out with the knife at the same time. The Cuban dodged the Bundi blade and shifted a leg to take the kick on his thigh. Encizo's knife swung low, slicing open his opponent's leg from ankle to knee.

The Indian screamed and slashed his Bundi dagger at the Cuban's face. Encizo moved his head and dipped his shoulder beneath the path of the blade. He executed a fencer's foil lunge and thrust the point of his Tanto under the Bundi man's extended arm. The Indian shrieked as sharp steel punctured his armpit, cutting into the nerve cluster. He dropped the Bundi dagger and fell to the ground, overpowered by shock and internal bleeding.

Not far away David McCarter blasted a bandit with his M-10 Ingram before the bastard could fire an Enfield .38 revolver. However another Indian low-life swung an old Mauser carbine like a baseball bat and clubbed the machine pistol out of the Briton's fingers. The bandit raised the carbine, planning to split Mc-Carter's skull with the buttstock.

The British ace sidestepped the attack, and the bandit swung the Mauser with all his might. As the shock struck a boulder and cracked in two, McCarter slashed the side of a hand into his attacker's left kidney and grabbed the man's hair. He yanked the Indian backward to ram a knee to the small of his opponent's back. The bandit tried to alter the grip on what remained of his carbine, hoping to strike out at the Briton who was now behind him.

McCarter shoved hard, slamming the Indian into the boulder. The broken Mauser slipped from the man's hands. McCarter held on to his assailant's hair and smashed his face into the merciless rock twice more before he released the outlaw. The Indian slumped to the ground unconscious, his front teeth shattered and his nose mashed into a bloody smear in the middle of his face.

Yakov Katzenelenbogen had laid down his Uzi and drew his SIG-Sauer pistol, fearful that the full-auto weapon might strike an ally during the fight at close quarters surrounded by a green cloud of smoke. Three bandits attacked the Israeli. One man held a pistol and the other two were Gurkhas armed with their deadly *ku-kri* knives.

Katz instinctively took out the pistol man first, pumping two 9mm rounds into the attacker's chest. The son of a bitch went down forever, but the two knife artists kept coming. Katz raised his SIG-Sauer and fired. A parabellum slug drilled through the closest Gurkha's forehead and literally stopped him dead in his tracks.

The other Gurkha got close enough to use his knife. He swung the murderous thirteen-inch blade at Katz's wrist, planning to chop the Israeli's left hand off with the gun still in it. Katz quickly moved his arm. The *kukri* missed its target, but grazed the Phoenix Force commander's left thigh. Katz grunted as blood oozed from the cut in his upper leg.

Yakov ignored the pain and chopped the butt of his SIG-Sauer down on the ulnar nerve in the Gurkha's forearm. The knife fell from the little killer's grasp. Katz quickly jammed the steel hook of his prosthesis under the Gurkha's jaw. The metal talons snapped around the man's throat. Katz pulled hard, tearing the Gurkha's trachea open and severing a carotid artery. The bandit dropped to the sand, his body twisting wildly as his life poured out on the ground.

Gary Manning had also been concerned about using a full-auto weapon at close quarters. The big Canadian found the long-barreled FN FAL awkward for hand-to-hand combat. However, he still held the FN FAL, his left fist around the stock just below the trigger mechanism. Manning held his .357 Colt revolver in his right hand as he confronted four charging bandits.

One opponent tried to lunge with a bayonet attached to the muzzle of his Lee Enfield rifle. Manning triggered two Magnum rounds and punched both 158-grain projectiles through the Indian goon's throat and mouth. The attacker collapsed in a dying lump. Another outlaw raised a scimitar, and Manning quickly shot the bandit under the chin, blasting a .357 slug through the roof of his mouth into his brain.

A Sikh renegade closed in and swung a large curved knife at the Canadian. Manning turned sharply and raised his left arm, swatting the buttstock of his FN FAL rifle into the third attacker's wrist. The knife hurled from the Sikh's hand. The bandit muttered something in Punjabi before Manning jabbed his left arm twice, stamping the butt of his rifle into his opponent's breastbone and the point of his chin.

The Sikh fell unconscious while the fourth and last bandit attacked with a hatchet held in both fists. Manning fired his Colt Magnum, blasting a .357 round into the aggressor's stomach. The psycho screamed in agony, but continued to charge. Manning stepped forward, raised his left arm and turned swiftly, lashing the barrel of his assault rifle across the hatchet man's forearms. The blow sent the ax hurling from numb fingers. The bandit staggered forward and tried to reach for Manning's throat with his bare hands.

"You get an A for effort," the Canadian rasped as he stabbed the muzzle of his FN FAL into the Indian's solar plexus and pulled the trigger.

The bandit gasped, vomiting blood from his bullet-ruptured stomach. He fell to his knees, choking to death on his own insides. Manning put him out of his misery with a well-placed .357 round through the left temple.

Robert Hislaw had managed to shoot and kill one charging bandit before he ran out of ammo in his Sterling subgun. The NSA man reached for his 1911 A-1 Colt, but another Indian leaped upon him before he could clear leather. The bandit struggled with Hislaw, trying to drive a short-bladed dagger under the agent's ribs.

Suddenly the bandit screamed and sprawled limply across Hislaw. The NSA operative shoved the Indian aside and stared down at the guy's twitching corpse. One of Encizo's *shaken* throwing stars was buried in the base of his skull.

"You okay, *amigo*?" the Cuban inquired as he helped Hislaw to his feet.

"Yeah," the agent replied breathlessly. "I don't think I'm cut out for this shit."

"If it was easy," McCarter said as he loaded a fresh magazine in the well of his Ingram, "anyone could do it."

"Hey, you guys down there!" a voice shouted from the rocks above. "This is Bahir Khan. You know who I am, yes?"

"We've heard of you," Katz yelled back as he limped to his Uzi. "You used to have a lot of bandits working for you, but most of them are dead now."

"You guys are tough." Bahir Khan admitted. "We've fought enough, yes? How about a truce before everybody kills everybody else?"

"We're willing to call it a draw," Katz assured him. "Of course, we need some assurance that you fellows won't bother us again."

"You have the word of Bahir Khan," the bandit chief announced.

"I like dealing with an honorable man," the Israeli replied. "Perhaps we can discuss a business arrangement."

"Business?" Bahir Khan's voice seemed surprised. "What sort of business?"

"Making a profit," Katz answered. "What other sort of business would be of interest to a mercenary?"

"Very well, my friend," the bandit said, laughing. "We shall talk."

17

"What the hell do you think you're doing, Jacobs?" Robert Hislaw demanded, stunned by Katz's invitation to Bahir Khan. "What do you want to talk to a cut-throat hill bandit for?"

"Exactly what I told him I wanted to talk about," the Phoenix Force commander replied. "A business deal."

"I don't think I have to tell you we can't trust a god-damn *bandido* chief," Encizo remarked, chambering a round in the breech of his MP-5. "Are you sure it's a good idea to make a deal with this hombre?"

"You said it yourself, Mr. Santos," Katz began, lighting a Camel cigarette. "We can't trust him. If we just let him ride off, he might head straight for the Thuggee stronghold. Somnoka said the bandits know these hills better than anyone else. That means Bahir Khan could probably reach the Thugs before we could find their headquarters, especially if we tried to find the base on our own."

"Oh, shit," Calvin James groaned. "You're not thinking of a deal to get these bandits to help us find the Thugs? Man, that's crazy. What's to stop them from turning on us when we find the base?"

"Look," Gary Manning said, pointing at a lone figure who descended a rock formation. "The guest of honor has arrived."

Bahir Khan climbed down the stony surface as easily as a man on a flight of stairs. The bandit leader wore canvas trousers and a dark green cotton shirt with a goat-skin vest. His boots were made of deer hide with rabbit fur around the ankles. The bandit carried two Enfield revolvers thrust in his belt. A large knife was sheathed at his right hip, and the brass handle of a scimitar jutted from a scabbard at his left.

Bahir Khan carried a pole over his right shoulder with a dirty white cloth tied to one end. He did not wave the crude flag, apparently confident the men of Phoenix Force would hold their fire. The bandit climbed to the base of the rock wall and held the banner forward.

"I am Bahir Khan," he announced. "I come in peace."

The bandit's face did not belong to a pacifist. A dark green turban was bound around his head. Bahir Khan's left cheek had been slashed by a knife, the scar extending from below his eye to his beard. His smile was confident, perhaps arrogant, and his pale hazel eyes revealed natural cunning and shrewdness.

"You may call me Jacobs, Bahir Khan," Yakov Katzenelenbogen declared. "I assure you that your white flag will be honored and we will respect your truce."

"If you fail to do so," the bandit replied with a smile, "I have men with rifles watching at this very moment."

"We rather assumed you did," Katz said with a shrug.

"You have been wounded, Mr. Jacobs," Bahir Khan remarked, noticing the crimson stain at Katz's thigh.

"Jesus," Calvin James, the unit medic rasped. "Let me take care of that, Yak...Jacobs."

"Later, my friend," Katz told him. "The wound is nothing. Had it been a couple inches higher, then I might have a real problem."

"This is so," Bahir Khan said, laughing. "Injury is not new to you, I see. Did you lose your arm in battle, as well?"

"In a war many years ago," Katz confirmed. "We are both veteran warriors, Bahir Khan. We do not make idle threats and accusations. That is the job of politicians. Nor do we lie about conditions of peace or terms of business agreements."

"Ah, business," the bandit smiled. "Now what sort of business shall we discuss? You said something about a profit, yes? Now that is interesting."

"Then let's get to business," the Israeli replied. "First, how much are the Russians paying you to protect their base and the Thuggees at the mountain of Kali?"

"The Russians?" Bahir Khan raised his eyebrows. "You are well informed, Mr. Jacobs."

"We try to be," Katz replied. "How much do the Russians pay you?"

"They're supposed to give me a hundred *tolas* of gold," Bahir Khan admitted. "So far, I've only received thirty."

"A hundred *tolas*." Katz frowned. "A *tola* is only about eleven grams, correct?"

"Eleven point seven to be exact," Bahir Khan answered.

"That's less than half a Krugerrand," the Israeli remarked. "We can double that. Two hundred *tolas* of gold ought to be an attractive offer."

"Very attractive," Bahir Khan said as he smiled. "I'd consider that ample compensation for the loss of my men. Of course, the Russians have already hired our services. Not very professional for us to cancel a deal after we've received partial payment in advance."

"The Russians only paid you thirty *tolas*," the Israeli commented. "They owed you that much for the men you lost today."

"This is true," the bandit agreed, easily accepting Katz's logic. "The Russians should have told us how well armed you fellows would be. I blame them for the deaths of my men. You were merely acting in self-defense."

"I'm glad you feel that way, Bahir Khan," the Phoenix Force commander stated. "But of course, if you're to earn two hundred *tolas* of gold, you'll have to help us accomplish our mission."

"And your mission is to launch an attack on the mountain of Kali?" The bandit chief frowned. "That is impossible."

"Nothing is impossible," Katz insisted. "Some things are just a bit more difficult than others."

"You don't know what the mountain of Kali is like," Bahir Khan told him. "The Russians are well armed, even better armed than you. They have machine guns and explosives and there are more of them. You would also have to deal with the Thuggees. They are total fanatics and very dangerous. Don't underestimate them because they do not carry guns, my friend."

"We've encountered Thugs before," Yakov said. "We know what they're like."

"There could be more than a hundred Thuggees at the mountain of Kali," Bahir Khan stated. "There are never less than thirty or forty assembled there."

"We'll take care of the Thugs and their Soviet allies," the Israeli assured him. "All we want you to do is help us find the base."

"You talk as if you've been there, Bahir Khan," Gary Manning remarked.

"I have been to the mountain of Kali," the bandit confirmed. "I have lived in these mountains all my life. My father was a tribal chief in the Benares during the occupation of the British. This is how I learned to speak English. Sometimes my father fought the British, sometimes he worked with them. My family has always recognized the need to remain flexible when dealing with others."

"Is your bleedin' biography leading somewhere or do you think we're really interested in your family history?" David McCarter asked, clearly annoyed.

"You're English, eh?" Bahir Khan smiled. "That's all right. I have no grudge against the British. My point is, I know these mountains very well. I knew the place that is now the mountain of Kali before the Russians came with their machines to dig through rock and build a tunnel inside the mountain. I can take you there, but I warn you it will be very dangerous. Some of my men will not assist us. They believe the Russians have brought some sort of dark magic with them. And they may be right. Very strange things happen at that place."

"Such as a living statue of the goddess Kali?" Katz inquired.

"Don't laugh, my friend," the bandit said grimly. "I saw it myself. I am a Moslem and I do not believe in the gods of the Hindus. My Gurkhas are Hindus, but they do not believe in the legend of Kali. Shiva is their main god. They no more believe that Shiva had a daughter than I believe that Allah had a son named Jesus."

"Then why does the mountain of Kali frighten them?" Encizo asked.

"If magic exists," Bahir Khan replied, "it is either the power of gods or devils. You can not kill a devil with a gun, my friends."

"Don't concern yourself with such matters," Katz stated. "All you have to do to earn two hundred *tolas* of gold is take us to the mountain of Kali. We'll take care of the rest, including the devils."

"You must think me a superstitious fool," Bahir Khan said with a sigh. "Men such as you do not believe in devils?"

"Evil exists," Katz remarked. "All of us have seen it being carried out by ambassadors of wanton destruction and senseless death. Many of these people are pawns of evil, but there is always someone responsible pulling the strings. Maybe these manipulators justify their actions by some sort of ideology that they genuinely believe excuses their conduct. But the results of this evil, the reality of it in actual practice, remain the same. So I guess we do believe in devils, Bahir Khan."

"Let me assemble what remains of my men," the bandit leader declared. "Then we shall discuss business in more detail."

18

Sergeant Kuznetsov noticed a large blip on the screen of the heat-sensor-activated land-radar scope. The Soviet military technician checked the location of the object and switched on the telescope surveillance equipment in that area. A radio-operated robot camera with a telescopic lens mounted at the peak of a tall rock formation slowly revolved on its pedestal.

"Gd'yee o'nee?" Kuznetsov wondered aloud. "Where are they?"

He watched the television monitor, viewing the terrain of the Benares mountain range through the eyes of the robot telescope two miles away from the Russian base. Kuznetsov saw only rocks and sand. The sergeant patiently waited for the camera to revolve a second time. A group of figures moving along a narrow pass appeared on the screen.

Sergeant Kuznetsov reported his discovery to Captain Tikhonov, the second in command of Operation Postcard. Tikhonov was an officer in the Glavnoye Razvedyvatelnoye Upravleniye or the Chief Intelligence Directorate. The GRU is part of the Soviet General Staff and functions as a military intelligence organization. Technically it is a separate outfit from the KGB, but more often than not the GRU acts as a mere extension of the KGB.

Captain Tikhonov had been chosen as second in command for Operation Postcard because a number of military personnel were involved. The Kremlin was showing token consideration to the General Staff by having a GRU officer in a position of alleged authority, but Tikhonov realized the KGB was really in charge. He resented this, and he despised Major Yousopov. The captain hated his assignment and he hated India.

"It's a bunch of *chernozhopy*," Tikhonov remarked as he looked at the eleven men on the TV screen. "Bahir Khan and his *chernozhopy*."

Tikhonov always referred to Indians as *chernozhopy*, the Russian equivalent of the term "niggers." Literally translated, this expression means "black ass." Tikhonov considered anyone who was a shade darker than himself to be *chernozhopy*.

"But Bahir Khan has more than fifty bandits under his command," Sergeant Kuznetsov commented. "I wonder if the rest of his men were killed fighting that special commando team the Americans sent."

"Don't be absurd," Tikhonov snorted. "There are only five Americans in that team, and one of them is a stinking *chernozhopy*. They couldn't possibly survive an ambush against ten-to-one odds."

"Perhaps not," Kuznetsov replied. "But they may have whittled down the number of bandits before Bahir Khan could kill them. After all, sir, it appears they wiped out all opposition at Ram Somnoka's palace."

"Well, it certainly looks as if those bandit trash are heading this way," Tikhonov admitted, gazing at the monitor. "Better inform our fearless leader from the KGB..."

"I'm already aware of what's happened, Captain," Major Yousopov said dryly, stepping behind Tikhonov. "But I'd like to see the monitor, please."

"Certainly, Major," Tikhonov said, stepping away from the screen.

Yousopov gazed at the monitor. The figures on the screen were dressed in peasant shirts, baggy trousers and dark turbans. Two men rode horses. The major recognized the rugged, bearded face of Bahir Khan. The bandit chief sat proudly in the saddle, leading his ragtag group.

"He shouldn't come here now," Yousopov said, frowning. "Nangal is preaching to a congregation of Thuggees. Bahir Khan was supposed to contact us by radio if he had anything to report."

"Perhaps his radio is not working, Comrade Major," Sergeant Kuznetsov suggested.

"Whatever the reason," Yousopov replied, "we can't allow that idiot to bring his men here during Thuggee services. Those fanatics would have a riot if a bunch of outsiders showed up. Captain, go through the emergency tunnel and stop Bahir Khan before he can get close enough to the Thugs to cause an incident."

"Me?" Tikhonov glared at the major. "Why send me? I don't speak their barbarian language."

"Bahir Khan speaks English," Yousopov replied. "According to your files, you also speak English fluently. I'm certain you two will have a nice little chat."

"Bahir Khan and his *chernozhopy* scum are cutthroat gangsters," the GRU captain complained. "Who knows what they might do? Those savages may have been using hashish or opium..."

"I'll send three of our best paratroopers to protect you, Captain," Yousopov said with a sigh. "But I want you to do something useful for a change. Go talk to Bahir Khan. That is a direct order, Comrade Captain."

"Da, Tovarich," the captain said with an angry salute.

CAPTAIN TIKHONOV and three Russian paratroopers marched across the dry rocky surface as the afternoon heat burned down at them. They were accustomed to the cold climate of the Soviet Union and the cool interior of the hidden base inside Kali mountain. Tikhonov mopped his sweaty face with a silk handkerchief and muttered complaints and curses under his breath. Damn Yousopov and damn the KGB and damn the son of a Ukrainian pig at the General Staff in Moscow who assigned him to such a miserable mission.

Half a mile from base, the four Russians found Bahir Khan and his group. Tikhonov groaned with disgust when he saw the bandits. It was humiliating to have to associate with subhuman garbage such as these, the captain thought. Even for the ultimate victory of international communism, this was too great a sacrifice to make.

"Bahir Khan," Tikhonov announced in a hard, commanding voice. "I order you to halt!"

"Who are you?" the bandit leader asked, sliding down from his horse. "You are not the man I usually talk to."

"That was my good fortune until today," the captain said gruffly, thankful for the three paratroopers armed with AKMS assault rifles. "You're not supposed to be here. Why haven't you followed orders and reported to us by radio?"

"My radio was broken in the battle with the Americans," Bahir Khan said with a shrug. "Most of my men were killed in the fight. See how few I have left...."

The bandit chief suddenly threw himself to the ground. Four of his men did likewise. However, the other six aimed weapons at the startled Russians. One of the paratroopers raised his AKMS. A figure with a green turban aimed a Browning Hi-Power equipped with a nine-inch silencer and squeezed the trigger twice.

The paratrooper cried out as two 9mm rounds smashed through the bridge of his nose and his right eye socket. The Russian soldier collapsed, his face covered with a veil of blood. The other two paratroopers tried to dive to the ground, hoping to return fire with their assault rifles. A bandit with an artificial arm and steel hooks for a right hand aimed a SIG-Sauer and fired a muffled round through its sound suppressor. A parabellum slug split the top of a Russian's skull before he could aim his rifle.

A tall black man stepped forward and aimed a Colt Commander as the last paratrooper put the wire stock of his AKMS to a shoulder. The black warrior's pistol rasped twice, and the Russian's face exploded.

Captain Tikhonov gasped in horror and fumbled for the button-flap holster on his hip. The GRU officer was trying to draw his Makarov automatic when a metal star hurled into his chest. Tikhonov fell to his knees, moaning in pain as blood trickled down his shirtfront. The black man approached him.

"Chernozhopy!" Tikhonov snarled with contempt as he yanked the Makarov from leather.

"Your mama," Calvin James replied.

He fired his pistol and pumped a .45 slug between the captain's eyes. Half of Tikhonov's head disappeared when the big 185-grain hollowpoint expanded at the back of his skull. James reached down and pried the *shaken* throwing star from the dead man's chest.

"By the Prophet's beard," Bahir Khan commented. "You fellows guessed right. The Russians did know we were coming."

"With all these peaks for observation points I'd be surprised if they didn't have spy cameras set up," Yakov Katzenelenbogen declared as he gathered up his Uzi. "Especially since the Soviets have had some of their top electronics personnel and robot technicians stationed here."

"Yeah," James remarked, handing the *shaken* to Rafael Encizo. "And the Ivans are probably watching us right now."

"Probably," the Cuban agreed, returning the star to a leather pouch on his belt. "But they'd find out eventually."

"That means we can expect a warm reception at Kali mountain," Gary Manning added.

"Well," David McCarter said with a shrug as he removed the silencer from his Browning pistol, "if you can't stand the heat..."

"Shit," Robert Hislaw muttered. "It's too late for me to get out of the kitchen now, but if I survive this crazy mission, I sure as hell plan to resign from the NSA. This is too much for me, man."

"I've done my part," Bahir Khan declared, climbing onto his horse. "My men and I are leaving now. If you fellows come out of here alive, don't forget the gold you owe me."

"We may even throw in an extra *tola* or two for a bonus," Katz assured him.

"May Allah bless you," the bandit chief said with a smile. "And if you die, may Allah give you a nice place in paradise."

19

High priest Nangal addressed almost a hundred Thuggees who had gathered at the base of the mountain of
Kali. He was leading the faithful in a series of chants
when the hearing-aid-style radio-receiver in his left ear
beeped twice. Nangal told the congregation Kali had
summoned him into the cave for holy guidance.

"The American commando team is approaching on
foot," Major Yousopov told Nangal when he met the
Indian in the tunnel. "They're less than half a mile
away."

"What is this?" Nangal glared at him. "How did they
get past your fancy security system? Why didn't you take
care of them before they got this close?"

"They were traveling with Bahir Khan, disguised as
members of his bandit gang," Yousopov explained. "I
sent Captain Tikhonov and an escort of soldiers to find
out what the bandits wanted. The Americans shot
them."

"I heard no shots," Nangal said. "The sound would
certainly carry within the rock walls of the valley."

"They used sound suppressors on their weapons," the
major answered. "We saw the whole incident on a
monitor."

"So put silencers on some of your guns and go kill them," Nangal told him. "I thought you Soviets were all trained to deal with defense by a strong offense."

"The Americans used silencers because they didn't want to announce their approach," Yousopov said. "But if we attack them now they'll probably use weapons without sound suppressors because they'll know we're already aware of their presence."

"But you're supposed to handle this sort of thing," Nangal insisted.

"If we engage in a shooting war with the Americans this close to the mountain of Kali, the Thuggees will hear it," Yousopov explained. "If they find Soviet troops in the area, they will demand to know why. Even those brainwashed fanatics would suspect that we were stationed nearby. That would directly connect us with your cult."

"So what do you want me to do?" Nangal asked.

"Tell your followers Kali has informed you that infidels are coming to attack them," Yousopov replied. "Tell them the goddess wants these nonbelievers destroyed."

"You want my people to be cannon fodder," Nangal complained. "The Thuggees are trained as stranglers. They aren't gunmen...."

"Even without firearms the Thugs could probably win against the Americans by sheer numbers," the major replied. "But it may not be necessary for all your followers to lay down their lives."

"But you don't want to risk the lives of any of your Russian comrades," Nangal sneered. "And you won't be outside when the Americans attack."

"No," Yousopov said with a smile. "But the goddess Kali will be out there."

PHOENIX FORCE AND ROBERT HISLAW approached the mountain of Kali. They were certain they had found their goal because they saw two figures at the mouth of a cave near the peak. One was a small Indian dressed in a yellow robe. The other was an incredible shape, seven feet tall with eight arms and a fierce bronze face.

"Holy shit," Robert Hislaw whispered as he gazed through a pair of Bushnell field glasses at the goddess standing beside Nangal. "You guys told me what to expect, but I can hardly believe I'm really seeing this."

"I know what you mean," Calvin James said, watching the arms of Kali moving in unison. "That thing looks like something right out of a nightmare, man."

"This is a nightmare," Gary Manning remarked grimly. "Now all we have to do is figure out how to end it."

"I hate to point this out," Rafael Encizo commented, "but we're getting a little low on ammo and it looks like the Thuggees are out in force."

"There must be more Russians around, too," David McCarter added. "But they're not going to come out of the woodwork unless they have to."

"Or out of the mountain of Kali," Yakov Katzenelenbogen remarked. "If we had a couple of rocket launchers we could probably flush them out."

"I knew I forgot to pack something before we left," Manning said with a shrug. "Guess we'll just have to get closer."

"Right," Katz agreed. "Try to use surrounding rocks for camouflage. We can't afford to handle the Thuggees with kid gloves, but we don't want to butcher the poor bastards, either. After all, they're only pawns of our real enemies. Religious extremists who have fallen victim to a clever con game."

"Those victims are goddamn killers," James muttered. "I damn near got throttled by three of those dudes back in Bombay, and I don't intend to let one of them get a scarf around my neck again."

"Who knows," McCarter said with a grin, "might be the start of a new fashion craze."

The commandos moved forward, stealthily darting from boulder to boulder. However, Nangal had alerted the Thuggees to watch for invaders. Too many eyes covered too great an area for Phoenix Force to advance unnoticed. Several Thuggees pointed at the assault team and shouted a warning to the others.

"That tears it," Katz muttered as the Thuggees charged like a human tidal wave.

The Israeli and Rafael Encizo opened fire with their Uzi and MP-5. They aimed low, firing a long burst of 9mm rounds at the Thuggees' legs. A dozen followers of Kali screamed and fell to the ground, their lower limbs shattered and bleeding, but dozens more kept coming.

Calvin James did not hesitate as he had in Bombay. The black warrior triggered a long burst of 5.56mm slugs that smashed into thighs and kneecaps. More crippled Thugs dropped shrieking to the dust. Two fanatics closed in, silk cords in their fists. James promptly shot both men in the chest.

Robert Hislaw did not show any consideration for the fact that the Thugs did not carry guns. He sprayed the charging horde with 9mm Sterling fire, pumping bullets into the attackers' torsos. The NSA man was too terrified by the maniacal assault even to consider shooting only to wound his opponents. Hislaw's sole concern was personal survival.

Gary Manning, the best rifle marksman of the lot, used his FN FAL with uncanny precision. He squeezed off 3-round bursts, smashing Thuggee limbs with 7.62mm rounds. The Canadian seemed almost casual as he picked off Kali fanatics, but his heart was racing with fear and excitement. The crazies charged on, running over the bodies of their wounded and dead comrades.

Three Thugs drew too close for Manning to risk firing a nonlethal shot. He raised the FN FAL and blasted two bullets through the nearest opponent's face. Another zealot lunged for the Canadian's neck with a twisted scarf. Manning quickly jammed the barrel of his rifle into the cloth garrote to block the attack. The Phoenix warrior swiftly slammed the buttstock of his FN FAL into the man's face, breaking his jaw.

The third Thuggee raised his scarf. Manning pivoted to face his attacker, but the would-be strangler vanished. The Canadian staggered back in astonishment. The Thuggee had not leaped away or ducked out of view. He had literally disappeared in a flash of blue-white light. Only a charred patch of ground remained where the man had stood.

"Jesus Christ!" Manning exclaimed.

"No," David McCarter rasped, his fingers poised on the pin of a concussion grenade. "It's Kali!"

The statue of Kali moved slowly, its necklace of skulls glowing like a monstrous firefly. Nangal stood clear of the eight-armed figure as he shouted down at the Thuggees.

"Stay back, my children!" the false prophet cried. "The mother goddess herself shall deal with these infidels!"

The Thuggees began to move away from Phoenix Force, and a bolt of fiery light flashed from Kali's necklace. The laser beam struck a boulder behind Encizo, and the rock dissolved instantly. The Cuban leaped away from the scorched earth where solid stone had been.

"Spread out!" Katz shouted. "Don't make it easy for them to zero in on a target!"

The Thuggees no longer presented a threat. The zealots turned their backs to the commandos, confident that their goddess would destroy the invaders. They gazed up at Kali and chanted to their deity as the skulls around the statue's neck began to glow once more.

Phoenix Force scrambled in different directions. Kali revolved slowly like the guns on a tank. The arms moved like a killer octopus waving its weapons in triumph. It extended the severed head in one fist as if using the ghastly ornament to help seek its quarry.

Enough of this shit, Calvin James thought as he raised his M-16 and triggered the M-203 attachment. The grenade launcher coughed violently, throwing a 40mm projectile at the mechanical monster at the mouth of the cave. The grenade struck below the ridge and exploded. The blast sent Kali tumbling over the edge.

Nangal screamed as the rock gave way beneath his feet. The high priest slid down the mountain and fell against a lip of stone. His thigh bone snapped, and a bone splinter ripped open flesh as Nangal howled in agony.

The figure of Kali plunged to the ground below, and the Thuggees wailed in horror and astonishment as they watched their goddess crash to earth. Metal arms burst from welded sockets. Circuits sparked and wires jutted from the broken statue. An arm jerked up and down woodenly, almost like the twitching motion of a dying creature.

"Hislaw!" Katz exclaimed. "Tell the Thuggees to look at Kali. See for themselves how they've been duped by liars who have used their faith for evil."

"I think they're figuring that out for themselves," Encizo remarked.

The Thuggees stared at the shattered remnants of Kali. None of them had ever seen a dead god before, but they realized the wires and tubes were part of something manmade. The stunned congregation gazed down at the thing they had worshiped. In the flickering of an instant, their dreams, future and faith had been crushed.

Then a new expression appeared on their faces. Their eyes burned with the hatred of betrayal. An angry, primitive cry burst from the throats of the followers of Kali as they rushed toward the mountain as if determined to tear it down with their bare hands.

The metallic rattle of a mounted machine gun suddenly erupted from the mouth of the cave. High-velocity bullets slashed into the charging Indians. At least ten collapsed, blood streaming from their bullet-riddled bodies.

"I think we found the Russians," McCarter commented, raising his Ingram.

"You won't get close enough to that machine-gun nest to use that thing," Manning told him as he adjusted the timing mechanism of a plastic disk.

The Canadian's arm whipped forward and hurled the plate in a high arch. The disk whirled straight into the mouth of the cave and exploded directly above the machine gunners. Three mutilated Russian soldiers erupted from the gap, along with a twisted chunk of metal that had formerly been a weapon.

Phoenix Force charged to the mountain of Kali. The Thuggees stayed back, frightened of the strangers who had arrived with weapons of fearsome might and the mysterious demons that lurked inside the cave. They were disoriented and confused.

McCarter and Encizo were the first to reach the mountain. Both men were experienced climbers and they quickly scaled the rock walls, easily finding hand- and footholds. Manning and James followed. The British and Cuban commandos reached the stone ledge where Nangal lay. The cult leader's smashed leg was covered with blood. He gazed up at the pair with helpless pleading in his tear-soaked eyes.

"Help me," Nangal begged. "Please..."

McCarter and Encizo ignored him and continued to climb higher. They heard voices shouting in Russian and boot leather scraping stone above them. The Briton braced himself against the rocks and extended an arm to Encizo. He held an SAS flash-bang grenade in his fist.

The Cuban took a hand from the rock and pulled the pin for his partner. McCarter nodded his thanks and lobbed the grenade over the ledge to the cave above. The concussion blast made the mountain tremble, but the Phoenix Force pros hung on. Screams echoed from inside the cave as Encizo and McCarter scrambled over the ledge.

Both men opened fire with machine pistols, blazing twin columns of parabellum rounds through the mouth of the cave. However, only one Russian trooper was still on his feet to receive a chestful of 9mm slugs. The others were sprawled on the floor of the cave, rendered senseless by the terrible force of the concussion explosion.

McCarter and Encizo waited for Manning and James to join them on the ledge before they advanced inside the cave to investigate the tunnel within. The control room was deserted except for the unconscious Sergeant Kuznetsov, who lay on the floor by the radar screen.

"You think we got them all?" Manning inquired softly.

"I don't know," McCarter replied. "If I built a setup like this I'd include a back door."

"Hey," James remarked. "Where's Katz?"

"Probably on the other side of the mountain," Encizo guessed. "Looking for the back door."

MAJOR YOUSOPOV AND LIEUTENANT KRONOV, a fellow KGB officer, had escaped through the emergency tunnel while their comrades fought the enemy. When the mechanical Kali had been destroyed and the machine-gun nest blown to bits, Yousopov realized the battle was lost. He also knew that any report to Moscow would be more favorable toward his survival if no one from the Soviet army could contradict his version of how the mission went sour.

When they emerged from the opposite side of the mountain, Yousopov tossed an F-1 hand grenade into the tunnel. The explosion dumped enough rock into the passage to block either Russians or Americans from following through the emergency exit.

"What do we do now, Comrade Major?" Kronov inquired.

"Raise your hands and surrender," Yakov Katzenelenbogen instructed as he stepped from behind a boulder, the Uzi braced across his prosthetic arm.

Yousopov opened his fist to drop a Makarov automatic. Kronov tossed aside his AKMS, turning his back to Katz. The young KGB officer quickly yanked a pistol from shoulder leather and whirled, hoping to catch the Phoenix Force commander off guard.

Katz triggered his Uzi and nailed Kronov in the chest with three parabellum rounds. Yousopov swiftly planted a boot in his slain comrade's backside before the dead man could fall. He kicked Kronov's corpse toward Katz and leaped for the Israeli's Uzi.

Katz shifted the aim of his subgun to avoid having the weapon knocked from his grasp by the body of Lieutenant Kronov. Yousopov's hands grabbed the Uzi behind the front sight. The KGB officer yanked hard and snapped his head forward, butting Katz in the forehead.

The Israeli's skull rang from the stunning blow. Yousopov wrenched the Uzi from Katz's fingers and tried to change his grip to trigger the submachine gun. Katz thrust a fast side kick to the Russian's kneecap. The joint cracked and Yousopov bellowed with pain.

The Phoenix commander lashed out with his steel hooks, slashing open Yousopov's left forearm. Then Katz chopped his steel prosthesis across the Russian's right wrist to knock the Uzi from his hand. The KGB major suddenly rammed a powerful shoulder to Yakov's chest and whipped a backfist across the Israeli's jawbone.

Katz staggered back three steps. Yousopov ground his teeth together as he painfully stood on the leg with a dislocated knee in order to launch a boot for Katz's groin. The Israeli blocked the kick with his left thigh, but the major's foot slammed into the knife wound in Katz's upper leg. The Israeli groaned as fresh blood oozed from the bandaged limb.

Yousopov dived forward, both hands aimed for Katz's throat. The Phoenix pro caught his opponent's arm, grabbing a sleeve with his left hand and digging his steel talons into biceps muscle. Katz fell backward, increasing Yousopov's forward momentum. He jammed a boot in the Russian's midsection and pumped his leg hard, sending Yousopov sailing overhead in a judo circle throw.

The KGB man hit the ground hard. Although winded and battered, Yousopov tried to rise. Katz got to his feet first, breathing hard, but holding up better than his opponent. The Russian reached for a rock or a fistful of dirt to throw in Katz's face. His fingers touched metal.

Yousopov smiled when he glanced down at the Makarov pistol. He scooped it up and swung the gun toward the Israeli. His smile vanished when he saw Katz had drawn the SIG-Sauer from shoulder leather.

As the KGB officer snapped off the safety catch of his pistol, Katzenelenbogen shot him between the eyes.

Maj. Mikhail Yousopov died swiftly; his body hardly trembled as life left it. Katz holstered his SIG-Sauer and gathered up the Uzi before returning to the other side of the mountain.

THE BATTLE WAS OVER. Phoenix Force claimed a handful of Russian prisoners but decided to let the Thuggees go. They were no longer Thuggees or believers in the goddess Kali. Katz wondered what it was like to actually see one's god destroyed before one's very eyes. What can one believe in after such an experience? Indeed, could one ever dare believe in anything again?

"The Russians had a hell of a radio set up inside that cave," Gary Manning told Yakov. "I managed to contact an NSA frequency Hislaw told me about. They'll arrange a couple of helicopters to take us back to Calcutta where the Indian CID will take the Russians off our hands."

"Did you remember to mention medical supplies?" Calvin James asked. "Some of these people are hurt pretty bad."

"They're going to send a medical unit," Manning answered. "At least we'll have some help cleaning up this mess."

"Then our mission is accomplished at last," Katz said. "By the way, what happened to Nangal, the phony prophet who was working for the KGB?"

"He's over there," Rafael Encizo answered, pointing at the base of the mountain. "The Thugs—or should I say former Thugs—yanked Nangal off the mountain and took out some of their frustrations on him."

Katz gazed down at the battered figure of Nangal. The former leader of the Cult of Kali lay motionless on the ground. His wrists were bound together at the small of his back by a knotted silk scarf. Another yellow cord bound his ankles together. A third Thuggee garrote was tightly bound around his neck. Nangal's face was almost purple and his tongue hung from his open mouth. The dead man's eyes stared up at the blazing sun without blinking.

"A bit of ironic justice," David McCarter remarked as he fired up a Players cigarette.

"Yes," Katz agreed wearily. "High priest Nangal is the last sacrifice of the Thuggees."

MORE GREAT ACTION COMING SOON

PHOENIX FORCE

#19 Sea of Savages

Pacific Powderkeg

A pair of renegade American Naval Intelligence traitors join forces with TRIO, the brutal Oriental crime syndicate, to steal a fortune in gold from a Colombian ship under U.S. protection. In a carefully planned and swiftly executed attack, the Colombian treasure craft is transformed into a floating coffin and stripped of its precious cargo. The aftermath resonates with a bitter accusation— the U.S. didn't do its job.

The President calls for "special action," and in a South Sea caldron, the warriors of Phoenix Force battle the pirates of a new age in a contest of wills that quickly becomes a bare-knuckled battle for survival.

Mack Bolan's

PHOENIX FORCE

by Gar Wilson

Schooled in guerrilla warfare, equipped with all the
latest lethal hardware, Phoenix Force battles the powers
of darkness in an endless crusade for freedom, justice
and the rights of the individual. Follow the adventures
of one of the legends of the genre. Phoenix Force is the
free world's foreign legion!

"Gar Wilson is excellent! Raw action attacks the reader
on every page."

—*Don Pendleton*

#1 Argentine Deadline
#2 Guerilla Games
#3 Atlantic Scramble
#4 Tigers of Justice
#5 The Fury Bombs
#6 White Hell
#7 Dragon's Kill
#8 Aswan Hellbox
#9 Ultimate Terror

#10 Korean Killground
#11 Return to Armageddon
#12 The Black Alchemists
#13 Harvest Hell
#14 Phoenix in Flames
#15 The Viper Factor
#16 No Rules, No Referee
#17 Welcome to the Feast
#18 Night of the Thuggee

Phoenix Force titles are available
wherever paperbacks are sold.

GOLD
EAGLE

GET READY FOR ACTION
with
THE GOLD EAGLE®
GEAR-UP FOR ADVENTURE
SWEEPSTAKES
Look for this sign

on special Sweepstakes editions
of **MACK BOLAN®**, **ABLE TEAM®**,
PHOENIX FORCE®, **TRACK®** and **SOBs®**
on sale at your bookseller in August.

First Prize: a 1986 Jeep® CJ
Second Prize: 10 pairs of sports
binoculars
Third Prize: 100 pairs of
Gold Eagle sunglasses

GUA–I

GET THE NEW WAR BOOK AND MACK BOLAN BUMPER STICKER FREE!

Mail this coupon today!